"I'm very, very attracted to you, Dyan."

Bending, Oliver lightly kissed her eyelids, her cheek, her lips.

Dyan lifted her hand and ran her fingertips over his mouth. "We hardly know each other," she said softly. "We only met a few days ago."

"Long enough to know that we like each other. Long enough to recognize the sexual attraction that we both feel. And don't say that it isn't there," Oliver added, capturing her hand. "You know it as well as I do."

"I wasn't going to deny it," Dyan admitted. "But..." She paused, seeking the right words, but Oliver finished the sentence for her.

"But you're not the kind of girl who goes with a man on the first date?"

SALLY WENTWORTH was born and raised in Hertfordshire, England, where she still lives, and started writing after attending an evening course. She is married and has one son. There is always a novel on the bedside table, but she also does craftwork, plays bridge and is the president of a National Trust group which goes to the ballet and theater regularly and to open-air concerts in the summer. Sometimes she doesn't know how she finds the time to write!

Books by Sally Wentworth

Sally WENTWORTH

One Night of Love

Harlequin Books

TORONTO • NEW YORK • LONDON
AMSTERDAM • PARIS • SYDNEY • HAMBURG
STOCKHOLM • ATHENS • TOKYO • MILAN
MADRID • WARSAW • BUDAPEST • AUCKLAND

ISBN 0-373-11810-4

ONE NIGHT OF LOVE

First North American Publication 1996.

CHAPTER ONE

THE signature beneath the letter from a leading
London insurance company was completely indeci-
pherable, but, thanks to his secretary's having neatly
typed his name, Dyan was able to read that the letter
was from Oliver Balfour, the man they were wishing
on her throughout the expedition. Dyan had a theory,
evolved from years of reading company letters, that
the higher up the hierarchical scale a man rose, the
less legible his signature became. And on that measure
this man must be close to the top.

Her mouth twisted into a little grimace when she
saw the terse command for the highly secret recovery
expedition to find the yacht, *Xanadu*, to start at once,
which, although it was put politely, was a definite
order. Didn't these people ever realise that there was
seasonal weather and the state of the tides to be taken
into consideration, for heaven's sake?

The rest of the correspondence about the ill-fated
Xanadu was in the file in one of their 'Top Secret'
metal boxes to which Dyan had been given the key
when her boss, Barney Starr, had handed her the
project. Before opening it, Dyan had locked herself
in her office and pulled down the blind, measures insisted on by Barney who had constant nightmares
about industrial espionage. In this case she thought
he might be overdoing it, because the *Xanadu* was
only a small vessel as ships went, but when she read
the list of missing artefacts sent by the insurance

company Dyan gave an incredulous whistle. It seemed that the motor yacht was the luxury toy of a millionaire pop-singer who had been over to Europe on a buying spree. Nothing wrong in that, except that he had been buying old and almost priceless objects: Russian icons, Fabergé eggs, Holbein miniatures, Greek and Egyptian funerary artefacts, a Roman statue... The list seemed to go on endlessly.

The millionaire had been taking them all back to adorn his new home in the West Indies, but a couple of days before they'd been due to arrive the boat had been caught in the tail end of a hurricane and capsized. The crew and passengers had got off and been rescued safely, but the boat had gone down in the Caribbean Sea. Probably because of the huge waterproof safe that had been built into it to house all the *objets d'art*, Dyan thought grimly as she studied the plan of the yacht. And raising that safe would be her problem, and that of the team she would pick to help her. Reaching out for the phone, Dyan began to put that team together.

Three weeks later, Dyan was standing in the airport in Nassau on New Providence island, waiting for the flight from London which was bringing Oliver Balfour to join them. She had worked extremely hard during those three weeks, getting the expedition ready to put to sea, but had done so with maximum efficiency and the minimum of fuss. It was important that no other salvage company should hear about the *Xanadu* and its cargo, so it was necessary to keep a low profile. She hadn't even told the crew what they were going after yet, letting them think it was a historic wreck. The only people who would know the truth were herself and the man from the insurers, whose plane,

she saw from the Arrivals board, had just touched
down on the runway.

Dyan wondered what he would be like, and didn't
look forward to meeting him. She would much rather
have handled the expedition on her own, without some
man from the insurers breathing down her neck. From
the wording of his letters Balfour sounded to be a
typically chauvinistic male, and she could just guess
at his reaction when he found out that there was a
woman in charge of the expedition. That he hadn't
been told she was a woman, Dyan was all too certain;
Barney, the head of the salvage company, had a
wicked sense of humour and he always found it extremely entertaining not to tell his customers that they
would be dealing with a female. When he spoke to
her, or spoke of her to a client, Barney always re-
ferred to her as just 'Logan', without any prefix, and
also conveniently dropped the pronoun. Often she'd
heard him on the phone saying, in his broad American
accent, 'I'm putting Logan in charge. One of my best
salvors, a qualified oceanographer. Logan will handle
it for you.' A couple of dozen times she'd seen the
customers' smiles of greeting slip into a look of
stunned surprise when they'd realised that 'Logan' was
a female. And not only female but also young, tall
and curvy, and with a mass of rich chestnut hair into
the bargain!

The customers' first impulse—and they were
without exception male—was to get on the phone to
Barney and demand to know what the hell was going
on. They were brusquely told that there was no sexual
discrimination in the Starr Marine and Salvage
Company, that Logan had been hand-picked for the
job and would do a good one. It had then been left

to Dyan to prove herself which, because she really was good at her job, she had always managed to do, but she still found it annoying, especially as she knew full well that if she'd been a man her proficiency would have been accepted without question. It was a matter of pride that every customer for whom she'd worked had asked for her by name if they'd needed to use the company again. But Oliver Balfour, of course, was a new customer and she fully expected to encounter the usual problems.

Picking up the jacket of the short-skirted linen suit she was wearing, Dyan hooked it over her shoulder and made her way down to where she was to meet Mr Balfour. A great many beautiful, long-legged girls passed through Nassau airport on their way to or from the holiday resorts, but even so Dyan attracted attention. It wasn't only her legs and that flaming hair; there was an air of cool confidence about her, in her walk and the proud set of her shoulders. It told anyone who cared to look that at twenty-six she had already made it, had got to where she wanted to be, and—apart from chauvinistic customers—no longer had to prove anything to anyone.

Dyan supposed that she could have dressed more conservatively for this meeting, made it less of a shock for the customer, but she didn't see why she should; it was her work that was supposed to be important, not her appearance. So she perched her sunspecs on the top of her head, fished the small sign saying 'STARR MARINE' from her bag and held it up in front of her as she waited for the passengers to come through.

She didn't expect to have to wait too long; the Club and Business Class passengers always came ahead, and she was quite sure her customer would be among them. A man was already emerging into the concourse, tall and carrying his one large bag himself. Dyan put him down as a returning local and looked past him for someone pushing a trolley loaded with enough luggage to last several weeks. But then she did a double-take as the man stopped in front of her and said, 'Are you looking for me? I'm Oliver Balfour.'

It wasn't often that Dyan had to tilt her head to look at a man, but she had to now, which must make him about six foot three, she judged. And so very English-looking in his well-cut dark business suit, worn regardless of West Indies heat. But what surprised her most about him was his youth. As he was a director of his company she had naturally expected him to be at least middle-aged, but this man looked quite young, only in his early thirties, his features still lean and clear-cut. And it was a good-looking face, which she also hadn't bargained for.

Taken aback by surprise, she hadn't answered, and he said on an impatient note, 'Well? Are you waiting for me or not?'

She gave him a hasty smile. 'Yes, I am. Welcome to Nassau, Mr Balfour.' She held out her hand. 'I'm Dyan Logan.'

Dyan looked at his face expectantly, waiting for realisation to dawn, for anger to take the place of shock, but to her surprise his brows merely drew together slightly for a moment and then cleared. Taking her hand, he shook it briefly. 'How do you do?' She blinked, expecting him to say more, but he merely added, 'Shall we go?'

'Er—yes, of course.' She smiled in genuine warmth, thinking in amazed pleasure that for once in her life she'd found a man who accepted women on equal terms. 'Is that all your luggage?'

'Yes.'

'You travel light,' she remarked.

'I try to.'

'I have a car waiting.' She started to lead the way, but paused to say, 'Do you need to change any money or anything while we're here at the airport?'

'No, thank you; that's all taken care of.'

She glanced at him with keen but hidden curiosity. He gave the impression of efficiency in that beautiful dark suit, and he looked very clean and neat, his dark hair trimmed to just the right length above his collar, his firm chin clean-shaven despite the long flight, and his nails newly manicured. With anyone else she would probably have reminded them that they wouldn't be near a bank or anything for some weeks, but with Oliver Balfour Dyan felt that it would be quite unnecessary; if he said it was taken care of, then that was it. Fleetingly she wondered how someone who looked so fastidious—there was no other word for it—would manage on board the salvage ship for a month or more. It was a fairly new vessel but definitely not in the luxury class.

They emerged from the airport into the heat of the day. It was May and the temperature was already up into the seventies. Dyan automatically slipped her sunspecs on and her companion crinkled his eyes against the glare of the late afternoon sun but made no move to put on any glasses. He strode along beside her, carrying his bag easily, a briefcase in his other hand. He was, Dyan realised, a big man, his shoulders correspondingly broad for his height, but the dark

suit played down his size, was so well cut that at first
glance he seemed merely lean and athletic.

In deference to his being the customer, Dyan had
brought an open-topped car rather than the pick-up.
He put his bag in the back and opened the door on
the driver's side. For a moment Dyan thought he in-
tended to drive, but it seemed it was merely good
manners, because he looked at her expectantly as he
held it open.

In that short skirt, Dyan showed a lot of leg as she
got into the low car. She gave Oliver a quick glance
under her lashes, interested to see whether it would
have any effect on him. He saw all right; he blinked,
but apart from that his face betrayed no emotion. The
typical cool Englishman, Dyan thought, her lips
twisting in intrigued amusement.

'Where are we going, Mrs Logan?' Oliver asked as
they set off.

'Well, you said in your letter that you were in a
hurry, so I thought we'd go straight to the boat. And
it's Miss not Mrs. But please, call me Dyan.'

He gave her a sharp look. 'Thank you.' And added
after a moment, 'Do you live in Nassau?'

'No. I'm only here because of your project.'
Glancing at him, she saw him frown a little, so said,
'Unless you'd like to drive round the island for a while
first? Have you ever been here before?'

'Yes, I have—and I'd rather go straight to the boat.'

'OK. Fine.' They fell silent and to break it she said,
'I hope you're pleased with the speed that we've got
the boat ready for you... Er—do you prefer to be
called Ollie or Oliver?'

There was a second of silence in which she could
almost hear him saying that he'd prefer Mr Balfour,

but then he said, 'Oliver will be fine.' Adding, 'I didn't
realise that the boat had been organised with any
special speed; I expected it to be ready by now.'

Dyan choked a little, thinking of the endless hours
she'd spent organising crew, provisions and
equipment. 'Oh, quite,' she said faintly.

'When will we actually leave?' Oliver asked.

'On tonight's tide. After dark, when there are fewer
people around. To maintain as much secrecy as
possible,' she explained.

'You seem to be fully informed about this expedition, Miss—Dyan?'

'Oh, yes, I am,' she hastened to assure him because
she'd detected a questioning note in his tone. 'Fully
informed on the whole project.'

'I see.'

She glanced at him again, wondering at the coldness
of his tone, but Oliver was looking out of the window
at one of the island policemen directing traffic in his
uniform of white shorts, shirt and helmet, and she
could learn nothing from his hard profile. They were
nearing the waterfront now and the streets were busy
with people and cars. Dyan concentrated on where
she was going and had no time to worry about Oliver
until she eventually drew up in the car park near the
dock where the boat was moored.

'This way,' she told him, and pointed down to the
end of the dock. 'The boat is called *Guiding Starr*.
Starr spelt with a double R, after Barney Starr, the
company head.'

'The salvage boat belongs to the company, then?
You haven't hired it?'

'No. The company owns all its own salvage vessels.
This one was being used to help recover part of an

oil-rig that had sunk in the North Atlantic, and had to be brought here and re-equipped for your project.' Dyan let that sink in, wanting him to know that the company had pulled out all the stops for him, but he made no comment.

There was no way you could call *Guiding Starr* a beautiful ship. It had a large after-deck fitted with cranes and other lifting gear, an enclosed area where they kept the submersible, and a high bridge below a mast that had so many electronic tracking devices attached to it that it resembled a junk yard. The hull was black, the upper bulwarks white. A ship built to do a special job with no concessions to gracefulness. Aboard, it was much the same. The cabins were small and practical, but very comfortable. The galley was fitted up with the latest gadgets, and there was a decent rest area with television and videos for the crew when they were off duty.

Dyan led the way up the gangway and on to the ship where Russ was waiting to welcome them.

'This is the captain, Russ Millar. Oliver Balfour,' Dyan introduced.

They shook hands, the eyes of both men flicking over the other, summing each other up as they exchanged polite greetings.

Dyan hid a small smile of amusement. 'I'll show you to your cabin,' she offered.

Oliver followed her below, apparently at home aboard a boat, ducking his head as they went down the companionway. Dyan opened the door of the cabin that had been set aside for him. It was one of the larger ones and should have been hers by rights, if the insurance company hadn't insisted on sending

Oliver along. Now, when Oliver stood inside it, the cabin suddenly seemed a whole lot smaller.

'I'm sorry,' Dyan apologised. 'The boat isn't really fitted out to carry passengers. But this is one of the largest cabins, and there's a bathroom opening off it.'

'You don't have to apologise; it's perfectly adequate,' Oliver told her, dropping his bag on to the bed.

'Great.' She smiled at him again. 'I'll leave you to unpack, then.'

She turned to go but Oliver said, 'Just a moment,' and she looked back expectantly. 'When am I going to meet the rest of the crew?'

'At dinner, I expect. We don't leave for a few hours yet, so I expect most of them are still on shore, making the most of being in port.'

'I'd like to see round the ship.'

'Of course. I'll take you round myself. I just have to go back ashore for a few things.'

'Shall we say half an hour, then?'

'Make it an hour,' Dyan said with a smile, the thought coming to her that she hadn't brought anything very glamorous in the way of clothes with her. Although that hadn't seemed important earlier.

The smile wasn't returned. 'Very well, an hour,' Oliver accepted, but with another frown.

'The steward's name is Joe. If you need anything just ring for him.'

Dyan left him in the cabin and hurried ashore, wondering if Oliver was always this austere. But a man who could so easily accept her as the head of the salvage project could, in her eyes, be forgiven a great deal. And there was something attractive about him, too, which was why she went to a boutique in the town and carefully selected a few new things for the voyage: a couple of dresses for the evenings and some new casual clothes, things she definitely wouldn't have bothered to buy if Oliver had turned out to be the middle-aged man she'd expected.

One of the crew was just going aboard as she got back to the ship and gave her a hand to carry her parcels, making her laugh as he tried to guess what was in them. Glancing up, Dyan saw a figure leaning over the ship's side, watching them, and recognised Oliver. He didn't return the wave she gave him, but raised the wrist that held his watch, letting her know that her hour was up. He had changed into lighter-weight clothes, but he still wore a tie.

Dyan gave the crewman the rest of her parcels. 'Drop these in my cabin for me, will you?' She walked over to Oliver and lifted a hand to push back her hair, blown by the evening breeze off the sea. 'Ready for the guided tour?'

His eyes were on her and this time he couldn't—or else didn't try—to hide the flicker of interest in them. 'Quite ready.'

She took him round the deck first, explaining what the equipment was used for, telling him she'd show him the submersible once they were out to sea.

'For security reasons?' he questioned, but said when she nodded, 'But surely anyone walking along the dock, or any boat passing by can see that this is a salvage ship?'

'Yes, of course.'

'And don't all salvage ships carry a submersible?'

'Yes, but not like this one,' Dyan told him, patting the covered underwater craft. 'This is specially for your project, and we prefer to keep it under wraps.'

Below again, she showed him the galley and the rest room, gestured forward. 'Those cabins are the crew's quarters.'

'How many are there in the crew?'

'Fourteen; seven people on each watch. Plus the cook, the steward, and ourselves.'

'You don't count yourself as crew, then?' he asked.

'No. I'm always on call.'

His eyebrows rose and Oliver was about to ask her a question, but she led the way into the operations room, the heart of the ship, where every gadget that had been invented to help in the search for underwater wrecks had been fitted. It was like an extremely modern computer room with a large chart table in its centre. Oliver walked into the room and looked round in fascinated interest.

'It's as you'd imagine the control deck of a spaceship to look,' he exclaimed.

'Yes, I suppose it is,' Dyan agreed.

He swung round to face her. 'You're obviously used to it. Do you know what all the machines are for?'

'Yes, of course,' she answered in surprise. 'This one, for instance, is the sonar. That's pulses of high-frequency sound that are bounced off the sea-bed,' she told him, getting her own back. 'The time taken for their echoes to return gives you the depth of the sea-bed at that point, so you can draw a map of the sea bottom. If there's anything unusual, a wreck or something, then it will show.'

'And you'll be able to recognise the boat we want from that?'

'No. It could be any wreck. Then we have to send down a submersible with a video camera to take a look.'

'Do people go down in the submersible?'

'Yes.'

'I'd very much like to go down some time.'

'It's really only for experienced divers,' Dyan started to explain.

But, 'I have diving experience. I told you I've been to the West Indies before; I took a diving course then.'

'Well, in that case, I'm sure we could arrange something,' Dyan smiled. There was a question which had been niggling at the back of her mind, and now, glancing at the bank of phones, she saw a way to answer it. Gesturing to them, she said, 'We're connected up to the international communications satellite; if you'd like to phone your wife and family, to tell them you've arrived safely, you can do it from here.'

'How very kind of you.' Oliver gave her a quizzical look in which she thought she noticed a touch of amusement. 'I'd like to use the phone some time— but there's no one waiting with breathless anxiety for me to call.'

'Oh. Fine.' Dyan turned away, feeling slightly abashed, which was totally unlike her. She glanced at her watch. 'It's almost time for dinner. We're eating early tonight so we can sail on the tide. Would you like a drink first?'

He nodded. 'Sounds a good idea.'

They went back to the rest room where Dyan poured the drinks herself and noted them in the book. Oliver asked her what it was and she explained that everyone entered the drinks they'd taken and settled up at the end of each voyage.

'Doesn't that encourage drunkenness?' Oliver questioned.

Dyan shook her head. 'Starr Marine doesn't employ drunks. Any crew member who got drunk would be put ashore at the next port; they all know that.'

'The men in the crew—I take it that they are all reliable and discreet?'

'Of course. They've been hand-picked for this project. They've all been with the company for some years and are seasoned sailors and divers.' That hadn't been what Oliver meant, but Dyan deliberately paused before she looked him straight in the eyes and added, 'They are all also honest men. You need have no fear that they'll steal anything they find.'

She had spoken stiffly, her tone cold, affronted by the implied insult to the men. But Oliver said, 'I'm more worried that they might be indiscreet, let fall information about the—about our quarry, so that another salvage company might get there first.'

'They haven't been told what we're going after. And as for where—well, no one knows that yet. You're supposed to be bringing that information with you,' she pointed out rather tartly.

Oliver nodded, but his eyes had drawn into a frown again.

A bell sounded. Russ came in with the first mate, followed by most of the crew. He introduced them to Oliver and they almost immediately moved into the galley for dinner. There were no set places; people sat round the long table where they pleased. Dyan would have sat next to Oliver, but she was still a little annoyed with him, although she supposed that he was bound to ask about the integrity of the crew given the nature of the salvage they were to raise. So she sat next to Hal, the head of the diving team, and let Oliver find a place next to the chief engineer.

There were four empty spaces round the table, those of crew members that they would be picking up in Antigua, local men who were taking advantage of their being in the area to take a break with their families. Dyan heard Oliver ask about the empty chairs and the chief engineer tell him that there were some men to come, but then Joe began to serve the food and nothing more was said. It was a good meal, made of fresh food and plenty of it. Not up to five star hotel standard, but very good for a Starr Marine boat. Dyan couldn't help glancing at Oliver to see his reaction, but he was apparently eating with as much appetite as the rest.

She only glanced at him a few times, and seemed to be giving her attention to Hal, who was recounting the story of his very first dive. But she had heard it all before and so her mind wandered, and naturally dwelt on Oliver, the stranger in their midst. He seemed a paradox; to be so open-minded that he had accepted her at once and without question, and at the same time anxious about the reliability of the men— men that he must know had been thoroughly vetted by Barney before they would be employed for a project such as this. And whatever his mind, his character wasn't open; he seemed to have a natural reserve, an air of reticence about him. The chief engineer was talking to him and Oliver was listening politely, but he glanced up before Dyan could look away and caught her eye. She gave him one of her warm smiles and he looked at her for a moment before nodding in return, but he didn't smile back. He didn't seem to smile much at all. Perhaps this is his first assignment, she thought excusingly. Perhaps he's too tense to relax.

His meal finished, Russ, the skipper, glanced at his watch and stood up, several other men doing the same. But those not on watch stayed in the cabin for coffee.

The boat made little noise as it put slowly out to sea, its modern engines hardly vibrating, the calmness of the harbour holding the boat steady. The curtains in the cabin were drawn and there were no passing lights to show that they were moving. Not until they were out of the harbour and into the open sea, when the engines were opened up, did a slight tremble along the decking betray that the boat was in its element at last.

Oliver felt it and looked up in sharp surprise. Putting down his coffee-cup, he said to Dyan, 'I'd like to talk to you, if I may?'

'Of course.' She stood up. 'Shall we go to the operations room?'

She walked ahead of him, her legs immediately adjusting to the movement of the ship, finding it no problem after so many salvage operations such as this. When they reached the ops room she waited until Oliver had followed her in and then closed the door behind them.

'This room is completely soundproof,' she told him reassuringly. 'I expect you want to give me the co-ordinates for the last known position of the *Xanadu*. All I know at the moment is that she went down off the Windward Islands.'

'No, that isn't what I want,' Oliver said tersely. 'What I want to know is just when your father is coming aboard?'

'My *father*?' She stared at him incredulously, thinking that she couldn't possibly have heard right.

'I haven't got a father—I mean, I did have one but he died years ago.'

'Well, your brother, then,' Oliver said impatiently. 'Whatever relation to you this man Logan is who's supposed to be in charge of this expedition. He should have been here from the start, but now I want to know exactly where he is.'

All the happy thoughts of a uniquely open-minded man faded abruptly. Dyan's face hardened. 'You'd better come with me,' she said shortly, and led the way into the office section where all the telephones were. Glancing at the clock, she calculated that Barney would still be in the office, hopefully having lunch . . . and hopefully the call would give him acute indigestion. She wrote the number down and gave it to Oliver. 'This is Barnaby Starr's private line in London. He'll be expecting your call. In fact, he's probably been waiting for it for the last four hours.'

She went to leave but Oliver lifted a restraining hand. 'Just a moment. Why should he be waiting for me to call? And where is Logan . . .?' Even as he said it the truth dawned on him. Oliver's eyes widened incredulously. 'You?' he exclaimed in utter disbelief.

'Yes, that's right. I'm in charge of this expedition, this ship, these men.' Her chin came up in angry challenge. 'And why not?'

Oliver's hand had automatically reached towards the telephone when she'd given him the number, but now his eyes were fixed on her face, his own still wide with shock. 'But I expected a——'

'A man,' Dyan finished for him. 'Of course you did.' Her tone was heavy with sarcasm, mostly because of her own disappointment.

Recovering quickly, Oliver's jaw hardened at her tone. 'Yes,' he agreed frankly, 'I was expecting a man. I was also expecting someone twice as old as you.'

'Really?' Dyan gave him a sardonic smile. 'You've turned out to be exactly the kind of male chauvinist *I* was expecting.' And then was immediately angry with herself for letting her feelings betray her into being rude.

And Oliver didn't let her get away with it. His eyes narrowing, he said tersely, 'A typically feminine and silly remark.'

Dyan's cheeks flushed a little. She should have apologised, she supposed, but was determined not to. Instead her chin came up and she said, 'You have two alternatives, Mr Balfour. You can either entrust me with your project, or we can turn the ship round, go back to port, and you can find yourself a new salvage company.'

'Or I could instruct Mr Starr to send out someone else to take charge of this expedition,' he reminded her shortly.

She shook her head decisively. 'No, you couldn't. Your contract with Starr Marine specified that they would supply an experienced and capable oceanographer to take charge of the operation. They've done that. If you don't want me, then that's your choice, but you will have to break the contract and go elsewhere.'

'That sounds suspiciously like blackmail,' Oliver said angrily.

With a shrug, Dyan said, 'I can't help the way it sounds. That's the way it is. Talk to Barney on the phone. Ask him for someone new. See what he says, if you don't believe me.'

She went to leave him alone in the office but Oliver, his eyes on her face, on the heightened colour in her cheeks and the angry fire in her green eyes, said, 'You don't sell yourself short, do you?'

'I don't have to. I know my job. Your project is no big deal from the point of view of finding and raising the *Xanadu*; it's only the nature of the cargo that makes it at all special.'

'Is that supposed to put me in my place?'

Dyan took a deep breath, striving to hold in check a temper that went with her hair. Usually she had no trouble; experience and responsibility had taught her self-control, and she was adult enough to know that disappointment was playing a great part in her emotions now. Balling her hands, she said as calmly as she could, 'No, it was meant to imply that I've done this job many times before—but you must already know that; Barney would have told you.'

'Yes, he did. But he left out one or two very relevant details,' Oliver said wryly.

'You mean he didn't tell you I wasn't a man.'

'Or how young you are.'

'Well, I'm afraid there's nothing I can do about either. You'll just have to make up your mind what *you* want to do.' She opened the door. 'I'll leave you to call Barney.'

'Wait.' His grey eyes regarded her thoughtfully. 'Does Starr ever tell the customers that you're a girl?'

'No.' She shook her head.

'Why not?'

'He has a twisted sense of humour,' she answered flippantly.

Oliver gave her a level look. 'Now tell me the real reason.'

Dyan met his eyes for a moment, then gave an angry gesture. 'Why do you think?' she said on a bitter note. 'If he did, I'd probably never get any work. Women don't usually do this kind of job, and men are naturally biased against women who encroach on what they consider to be their world. If I were a subordinate it would be OK, but they neither like nor trust a woman who's in charge.'

'You're talking about the company's customers?'

'Yes, of course.'

'What about the men in the crew?' Oliver said. 'Do they resent you?'

'No. We've all worked together before. They do their jobs, and I do mine.'

'But do they trust you?'

She saw what he was getting at. 'Yes, they trust me. They have to. Their lives are in my hands, are my responsibility.'

Again he gave her a thoughtful look. 'During dinner—they didn't seem to treat you as their boss, show you any deference.'

Dyan could see why he was doubtful, but it was difficult to explain to a stranger. Perching on the edge of the desk, she said, gesturing expressively with her hands, 'It's different on the sea. When we're down in the galley we're all shipmates together. But when Russ is on the bridge, then he's the captain and the men jump to obey him. And when we're diving, then Hal is in charge and his orders have to be obeyed. But I'm in overall command of the whole project, and I tell the ship where to go and the men when and where to dive. But they know I'm an expert at my job, that I know the sea. And they respect that. Just as I respect their expertise in their own particular fields.'

She paused, wondering if he understood. Oliver was watching and listening closely, his attention centred on her, and she knew that he did, that he was intelligent enough to imagine how it must be.

Dyan went on, 'There has to be someone who's experienced in wet salvage who is in control of the project. I'm that someone because I *am* experienced, because I'm a professional oceanographer and perfectly capable of undertaking this expedition. That I'm a woman shouldn't matter,' she said on a forceful note. But then gave a bitter little laugh. 'But it does matter, of course. Because all the rest counts for less than nothing where male prejudice is concerned.'

'I don't like being made a fool of,' Oliver said grimly.

'And I don't like being treated as a second-class citizen,' she retorted.

This time when she made for the door Oliver didn't try to stop her.

Glancing back briefly, she said, 'I'll be up on deck when you've made your call.'

But once outside the room, out of his sight, Dyan leaned against the wall for a moment, fists clenched, eyes closed, trying to regain some degree of composure. What the hell was the matter with her? she wondered, angry that she'd let it get to her. This had happened to her many times before but she'd seldom felt this uptight about it. But there was nothing more she could do. Oliver would either agree to go on or they would go back. But she had the sick feeling that this was one customer she was going to lose. He had been so convinced a man would be in charge that it hadn't even occurred to him that it might be her. Oliver had merely marked her down, first as 'Logan's' wife, then his daughter or sister. What she had thought was open-mindedness was in reality a mind so closed that it hadn't even contemplated the possibility of her being the boss.

On a sudden surge of anger, Dyan went into her cabin, picked up the parcels of new clothes that she'd bought, and threw them, with as much force as she could find, against the far wall. The boxes burst open, the flowing silk of dresses and underwear, the bright cottons of swimsuits and shirts spilling over the floor and furniture. Feeling a little better, but not much, Dyan went up on deck.

Oliver joined her much sooner than she expected him to. She was standing in the bow of the boat, looking out at the velvety blackness of the night, pin-pricked by stars and lights from the distant islands. The wind caught her hair, tendrils of it hiding her face, for which she was glad. Oliver came up to her but she didn't look round.

'That didn't take long,' she commented wryly. 'I take it we're turning back?'

Leaning an arm on the rail, Oliver said, 'I didn't make the call.'

Dyan stiffened her shoulders. 'You had already decided, then,' she said flatly.

'Yes—but to go on, not to turn back.'

That brought her swiftly round to face him, an impatient hand going up to push her hair aside. 'You mean you're willing to trust me—and without consulting Barney?' Her voice was full of surprise, and there was a flare of hope in her eyes.

Oliver nodded, and suddenly grinned, the unexpected smile so transforming his face that he seemed like an entirely different man. 'I thought we'd leave him waiting by the phone, wondering what the hell's happening.'

'Thanks,' Dyan said in husky gratitude. 'It usually takes Barney about an hour of persuasion before a new customer will give me a try,' she confided, on a sudden wave of happiness.

Oliver spread his hands. 'I recognise a *fait accompli* when I see it. I don't like the way it was done,' he paused, his eyes resting on her, 'but I'm willing to give you a try—Logan.'

Dyan laughed, said goodnight, and went down to her cabin to pick up all the new clothes and carefully hang them in the wardrobe.

CHAPTER TWO

THERE was no set time for breakfast on board the ship. Those of the crew who weren't on watch went to the galley when they felt like it, or when they were no longer able to resist the savoury smells of frying bacon and hash browns. Dyan usually contented herself with fresh orange juice and toast, so often had her breakfast in her cabin, brought to her by Joe. But on their first morning at sea she went down to join the others. Today she was wearing what she described as her working clothes; a pair of shorts and a loose, short-sleeved shirt, and a pair of yellow canvas espadrilles on her feet, but today the clothes were new. Her hair she had woven from the top of her head into one thick plait that she'd fastened with a yellow bow, although ordinarily she would have used just an elastic band. And ordinarily her face would have been clean of make-up, because there was no way she wanted to be seen by the men as a sex object, but today she'd looked at her bare face in the mirror and impulsively added enough make-up to enhance her appearance.

It was still early and most of the crew were in the galley, but Oliver wasn't there. He came in about ten minutes later, looking as if he hadn't slept very well. All the other men, without exception, were wearing shorts, but he had on a pair of lightweight trousers, although he had put on a short-sleeved shirt. Dyan was sitting at a table with Russ, and after helping himself from the buffet Oliver came over to join them.

28

'Good morning.'

Russ gave him a nod, but Dyan smiled at him and said, 'You look as if you're suffering from jet lag or something.'

'Probably,' he agreed. 'My body clock hasn't caught up yet.' He looked at her. 'I didn't give you the co-ordinates you wanted last night.'

'That's OK. There's plenty of time. We have to go to Antigua first to pick up some more members of the crew. That's where we're heading now. So you can count this part of the trip as a pleasure cruise,' she said lightly.

'I've never been the kind of person who goes on a leisurely cruise,' Oliver remarked. 'Not enough to do.'

'Why not go up and have a look round the bridge? I'm sure Russ will be pleased to show you round.'

'We already did that last night,' Russ remarked. 'After you'd gone down to your cabin.'

Dyan glanced at Oliver, guessing immediately that he'd gone to talk to Russ about her; to find out if she really was respected by the crew, if she really did know her job as she'd claimed. His face was impassive, but the fact that he showed no emotion told its own story.

'I hope you were reassured?' she said lightly.

He raised an eyebrow. 'Reassured?'

'If I were in your position I'd do some checking, too.'

'I told him I'd as soon sail under your command as any other expedition leader in the company,' Russ said brusquely.

She smiled her thanks at him and stood up. 'If you'll excuse me, gentlemen.'

Russ only nodded, but Oliver stood up politely. Dyan glanced at him as she went by, but his eyes were on her legs, which didn't altogether displease her.

Dyan went to the ops room to carry out the daily checks, mark up the logs. Her first concern was to see what other craft were in the area, to make sure that they weren't being followed. But they were still too near the islands and there were too many blips on the screen to be certain one way or the other. It wouldn't be until they'd left Antigua behind and were out of the main traffic lanes that they could check for sure.

A beeper sounded and Dyan went into the office to answer the phone. Without waiting for the caller to speak, she said, 'Hi, Barney. Have you got any nails left?'

'No nails, no fingers,' he replied cheerfully. 'What happened; didn't Balfour show?'

'There are some people, Barney, who believe in the equality of the sexes.'

'Yeah—mostly women. You talk him into it yourself?'

'Something like that.'

'Define "something".'

'We were already at sea before he realised,' Dyan admitted.

Barney gave a shout of laughter. 'Nice one, Logan. But if you have any trouble, put him on to me.'

'I don't somehow think that will be necessary.'

'Is that so? Balfour's fallen for that luscious body of yours, has he?'

Glancing through the glass partition, Dyan saw that Oliver had come into the ops room in search of her, and was profoundly grateful that the partition was soundproof. 'He appreciates my mind,' she said primly.

That brought another roar of laughter. Barney was a tease and enjoyed trying to discomfit her, although she'd long ago got his measure. He might make chauvinistic remarks but she knew that he was proud of her in his way and would give her all the protection she might need. He gave the impression of being tough, a rough diamond, but she knew that he was just a marshmallow below a hard crust.

'The guy must be a nut, then,' he told her. 'Or is he one of those?'

Dyan knew what he meant and said with certainty, 'Oh, no, he definitely isn't like that.'

'He's not, huh? Now how come you're so sure, I wonder?' Dyan didn't reply and he chuckled richly. 'Well, just remember, kid; if you're going to mix business with pleasure, then business comes first. OK?'

'OK, boss. I'll remember.' And Dyan put down the phone to go to join Oliver.

But as she stood up he came into the office. 'I've brought you the co-ordinates you wanted. And a report from the captain of the *Xanadu* on the sinking.'

Dyan glanced at the latitude and longitude figures he handed her and she gave a small frown. 'Would you like to see where this is on the chart?'

'Yes, I'd be interested.'

She opened the safe, put in the papers he'd given her, including the lat. and long. figures, carefully closed it again, and took him into the ops room.

'Take a break for ten minutes, Ed,' she said to the man bending over the radar screen.

The seaman left and she went over to the central chart table, sorted through the rolled charts beneath it, selected one, and laid it out on the table. 'The position you've given me is to the west of the Windward Islands, in the Lesser Antilles. The sea there isn't the deepest in the Caribbean, but it can be quite deep. We'll just have to hope the *Xanadu* is in shallow water. The boat was on its way to Jamaica, wasn't it?'

'Yes, but the pop star stopped off to live it up for a few days in Barbados, then got caught in a hurricane. When is the hurricane season out here, by the way?'

'From May to November.'

'Now, then?'

'Yes.' Dyan glanced at him, wondering if he was afraid. 'But we'll get plenty of warning from the National Hurricane Centre if there's one due,' she said reassuringly, testing him.

Oliver looked surprised so she knew she had been wrong. 'Then surely the captain of the *Xanadu* would have been warned?' he observed.

'Yes. But your pop star might have decided he was bored in Barbados and wanted to head for home.'

'But couldn't the captain have refused if he thought it was dangerous?'

'That might have depended on whether he wanted to keep his job,' Dyan said drily. 'Boat captains are at the whim of the owners. And he might have thought it was worth taking the risk. Late hurricanes are sometimes not much worse than a bad storm, and it could have gone in a different direction. Hurricanes are often capricious. They were unlucky to hit it. And having that heavy safe full of cargo aboard would have made it difficult for them to outrun the storm.'

'Do you think you'll be able to raise the boat?'

'That depends on whether we can find it.'

'But you have its last position.'

'That's not really much help,' Dyan told him. 'That could have been the *Xanadu's* last known position before it hit the hurricane, and it could have been blown a long way from there before it sank. I'll have to read the captain's report to find out. Then again, the captain might have deliberately given us the wrong co-ordinates.'

Oliver's eyebrows rose, his mind working fast. 'You mean he might be indulging in some private enterprise?'

She nodded, pleased by his quickness. 'Yes. Your pop star might have blamed him for the sinking and dismissed him without a reference. The captain could be out here right now, with another salvage vessel.'

'He isn't *my* pop star,' Oliver pointed out, then shuddered. 'God forbid.'

'As bad as that?' Dyan asked with a laugh.

'Worse,' he said with feeling. Then frowned as he said, 'So we might not find the *Xanadu* at all.'

'Or we might find it with the cargo already taken.'

'You paint a grim prospect,' Oliver said wryly.

'It might not be that bad. It rather depends on the pop star's intelligence and the crew's loyalty. If he kept on the captain and crew, is employing them on another boat, then everything will probably be fine. But it might be worth checking on that point.'

'I'll see to it,' Oliver said decisively.

She straightened up and found herself very close to him. His aftershave, fresh and tangy, filled her senses. For a moment she drank it in, but then their bare arms touched, and it so disturbed her that Dyan quickly moved away. She went to roll up the chart, but Oliver said, 'Just a moment. You had a rough idea of where we were heading so why did you start the voyage at Nassau and not somewhere nearer?'

'Because it was easier to equip the boat there. Because it gives us more time to see if we're being followed. Because we had to pick up the new submersible there. Because——'

Oliver held up a hand and gave her one of his transfiguring smiles. 'I think I get the message. Sorry I asked.'

Dyan smiled in return. 'Not at all. As the hirer you have the right to ask any questions you want.'

'I have?' His grey eyes met hers. 'Then tell me: what is a nice girl like you doing in a job like this?'

She gave a gurgle of amused laughter. 'That's a long story.' There was a knock on the door as the crewman returned. Quickly she rolled up the chart and stowed it with the others. 'OK, Ed,' she called out.

The sailor came in and took his seat at the radar screen. Dyan indicated the office and said to Oliver, 'I'll leave you to make your call.'

She went up on deck, to the area which the crew used to relax and sunbathe. Most of them sprawled out on the deck itself, lying or sitting on towels as they sunbathed or played cards. Dyan, though, merited one of the deckchairs and she stretched out on it with a magazine.

Russ saw her from the bridge and came down to join her, a couple of cans of beer in his hands. He gave her one and said, 'Where's the landlubber?'

'Phoning London. Checking on the captain of the boat we're looking for.'

He nodded. 'What do you think of this guy?'

'Too early to tell,' Dyan said off-handedly. She remembered her earlier flare of emotion, and wasn't at all sure that she wanted to discuss Oliver, but Russ obviously did, so she said, 'How does he strike you?'

'Different from the ones we usually get. Not standoffish, but he doesn't immediately try to be one of the guys, same as some of them do. I think he'll be OK.'

Russ wasn't a talkative man. Close to fifty, he was an American who had spent most of his life at sea, and loved it. Dyan had never seen him panic whatever the weather, probably because he had a great respect for the ocean and its sudden, dangerous changeability. And he was never irritated by the days of sailing up and down, searching the sea-bed, or dismayed by the orders she gave him to take the boat into tricky positions: close to barrier reefs or near to cliffs that towered over them. He was a seaman through and through. And a good judge of men; if he said that Oliver was OK, then that meant a great deal.

Leaning back, companionably drinking her beer from the can, Dyan wasn't at all sure of her own opinion on Oliver. Her hopes about him had been raised too high to start with, then dashed too low. But that had been mainly her own fault, she realised. It had been a mistake to be so pleased at the thought of finding an unprejudiced man; if she'd been more wary, then she wouldn't have been so disappointed to find that he was just as chauvinistic as the next man. So, she thought pensively, maybe it would be a good idea to look at him afresh. Start again from the beginning, so to speak. Taking a sip of drink, she pictured Oliver in her mind, remembering her surprise at his comparative youth and good looks when she first saw him. And she smiled to herself as she recalled how it had been important to find out whether or not he was married. Not that she particularly believed in marriage; she'd been disillusioned about that in the past, but she had to admit she'd been glad when Oliver had made it quite clear that he was unattached.

'You're smiling wider than a Cheshire cat,' Russ remarked mockingly. 'What are you thinking about?'

'My next leave,' she told him, knowing him well enough to be pert.

But he wasn't deceived. 'Watch your step with this guy,' he cautioned. 'Remember the last time.'

The glow faded from her face. 'You don't have to remind me,' she said shortly.

Putting a hand on her knee, Russ leaned forward to look into her face. 'I just don't want to see you hurt again. Are you over that bum?'

She nodded. 'It was nearly a year ago.'

'Good.' Russ waved an admonitory finger at her. 'But you be careful. You know how susceptible you are to English guys. I don't know how many times I've told you to go for a red-blooded American.'

Dyan laughed. 'Like you, I suppose?'

'Sure, like me.'

As, like Barney Starr, Russ had treated her like a daughter since she'd known him, Dyan knew that he was kidding as usual. Bending forward, she planted a kiss on his weathered cheek and said, 'I could never find anyone half as sexy as you, Russ.'

He laughed, enjoying the game they played, but someone gave a polite cough behind her and they both looked round to see that Oliver had come up to them.

Russ finished his drink and stood up. 'Time I was going back to the bridge.' He gestured to the chair he'd been using. 'Here, take a seat.'

Oliver thanked him and sat down beside her. Dyan was intrigued to see that he had changed into shorts. Compared to the rest of the crew, his skin was pale, but it was by no means lily-white. His legs were strong and muscular, as if he played a lot of sport, and, thankfully, not too hairy. There were one or two members of the crew who looked one step up from a gorilla. Some girls might like that, but Dyan found it a turn-off.

'Did you find out anything?' she asked.

'Yes. Hopefully we're in luck. The pop star has bought another boat, did so almost immediately, in fact—evidently it isn't good for his image to be without a yacht—and he kept on the captain and the original crew. It seems they rescued him when the *Xanadu* went down, so he's grateful to them for saving him to make more, and yet more music,' he said with a mock groan.

'Does he have his life insured with you?' Dyan asked in some amusement.

Oliver grinned back, 'Unfortunately, yes.'

'You should be glad, then.'

'Have you ever *heard* his so-called music, Dyan?'

'I think there are probably a couple of his cassettes on board,' she admitted.

'Then, please, I beg of you, don't play them when I'm around, or they'll end up over the side,' Oliver said feelingly.

She laughed delightedly. 'I'll tell Russ to give a top priority order to the crew.'

Joe came out on the deck carrying two tall glasses on a tray. 'I thought you might like a martini,' Oliver told her.

Usually Joe just brought up cans of cold beer, but these glasses were frosted and there was ice and lemon. He had evidently been given specific instructions. Dyan took one, hoping Oliver hadn't seen the empty beer can under her chair. He must, she thought, be used to living in a very civilised style.

'Thanks, that was thoughtful of you.'

'I had an ulterior motive,' he told her.

'Oh?' She gave him a half intrigued, half wary look.

'Yes. I thought you might get thirsty telling me that long story of how you come to be in charge of "this expedition, this ship and these men", if I remember your words correctly.'

'Oh, dear, was I as bad as that?' Dyan gave him a guilty look, but there was also amusement in her green eyes.

'Much worse,' Oliver returned and leant back comfortably. 'So?'

Dyan hesitated, wondering why he wanted to know. Was it out of genuine interest—or was he still checking up on her? Hoping it was the former, she said, 'I've always been fascinated by the sea. When I was small we had a house near the coast. My father loved to sail and he taught me. But I didn't want to just sail on it, I wanted to find out everything about the sea: what made the tides and the storms, what lived in it, what was down on the sea-bed. So, as soon as I was old enough, I went to college and studied oceanography.'

'And did well, obviously.'

She admitted that with a small shrug. 'There are four branches of oceanography. I studied all of them, but specialised in marine geology and marine ecology.'

'What are the other two?' Oliver asked, his eyes full of interest.

Dyan liked the way he seemed to give her his whole attention when he listened; his eyes stayed on her, he didn't look away as people often did when she talked about her work. 'They are the study of the physical, and the chemical components of sea-water. Marine ecology concerns the plants and animals you find in the sea, and marine geology is the study of the structure, features and evolution of the ocean basins.' She paused. 'I hope that didn't sound too much like a lecture.'

'No, it didn't. I suppose, in your job, you find the latter discipline the most useful?'

'Yes.'

'Where did you go to college?'

'Oxford first, then I came over to America, to California for a year.'

'And then you applied for the job with Starr Marine?'

'No.' Dyan shook her head. 'First I took an engineering course so that I'd understand about lifting gear and weight ratios, that kind of thing.' She frowned. 'Why are you shaking your head?'

He didn't answer directly, instead saying, 'Are there many women in this business?'

'I suppose you mean out at sea, actually supervising a salvage operation?' Not waiting for him to answer, she said, 'I'm the only one in Starr Marine at the moment, but there are other women coming into the job in other companies.' She gave him a direct look. 'Are you thinking that I'm the token woman, taken on to keep the Equal Opportunities Board happy?'

He gave her a lazy kind of look. 'Are you?'

Perhaps Dyan should have been annoyed by that question, but she had just noticed how long and thick Oliver's eyelashes were. She paused, having to gather her thoughts again, then decided to say teasingly, 'Maybe I am. You'll just have to find out, won't you?'

'I'm always reading that, to get anywhere in a man's world, a woman has to be twice as good at the job than the average male,' he commented. 'And somehow I don't think Barney Starr would risk his reputation by taking on someone who isn't competent to do the work just to please a pack of officials.'

'If that was supposed to be a compliment, it was so subtle that it hardly came across.'

Oliver laughed, his eyes arrested, and Dyan knew, with a surge of pleasurable excitement, that he was intrigued by her. But the warmth of the feeling brought her up short; after the last time, when she'd been so badly hurt, she had sworn off men. And Russ hadn't had to warn her to be careful, she had known herself that falling for the wrong man was a big mistake. But how was she to have known that Crispin had just been using her for sex, that he had lied when he said he wasn't married?

Taking a mental grip of herself, Dyan pushed the memories back into the deepest recess of her mind; not all men were the same, they weren't all two-timing swine. But when you'd been hurt once—well, then you were always far more cautious in the future. So she put the brakes on where Oliver was concerned, and said in a calm, almost businesslike way, 'How about you? How did you get into your job?'

Oliver shrugged. 'Much the same way as you. University and then one or two special courses. But insurance is humdrum compared to this. Have you taken part in many exciting salvage operations?'

So he didn't want to talk about himself. Through modesty, she wondered, or something else?

'Quite a few,' she answered. 'Especially when I was working my way up through the company. My first job was to help raise an oil-rig.' She started to tell him about it, making it sound interesting—because it had been interesting, and exciting at moments when it got dangerous. Again he listened intently, so Dyan went on to tell him of other salvage projects that she'd been involved with, ending, 'But once I'd served my apprenticeship, so to speak, and took on jobs of my own, they've all been wet salvage, like this trip.'

' "Wet salvage"?' Oliver's eyebrows went up.

'Oh, sorry. Dry salvage is when you have to rescue a vessel that's still afloat; wet salvage is when it has already sunk.'

'I see. And where is your base?'

'In London. But I'm not there very often.'

'But you have a place to live when you're not at sea?'

Dyan hesitated briefly, then said, 'I have an aunt who lives in Highgate, near the cemetery where Karl Marx is buried, and she lets me have a room.' She didn't tell him about the flat that Crispin had rented for her, where she'd lived with him in the assurance that he loved her, that they would be married one day. And which she'd walked out of the moment she'd found out that he had lied to her all along. But that was getting on dangerous ground again. 'Do *you* live in London?'

'Yes, I have a flat in Chelsea.' For the first time he opened up a little, saying, 'But my parents live in the country and I escape there as often as I can.'

'Do you ever go sailing?'

'I haven't done much,' he admitted. 'Mostly on holidays. I did some when I was out in the West Indies before, when I learnt to dive.'

They talked sailing and diving for a while, and Dyan found Oliver a good conversationalist. When he opened up on a subject he made it interesting and often amusing, but she sensed that he had barriers which he wouldn't let down lightly. But then so had she; not just barriers but stone walls with red warning signs all along the top of them.

But, when she eventually went down to the ops room to check the log, Dyan had to admit that the couple of hours she was on deck with Oliver had been the most pleasant she'd spent for quite some while. And not only because she'd enjoyed talking to him; being a woman, she'd known instinctively that he found her attractive. Whether he, as a man, had known the same about her, Dyan wasn't so sure. She'd tried not to give him any encouragement, to put out any vibes. Once bitten had made her more than twice shy, and there was no way she wanted to go rushing headlong into another relationship, another love affair. She had thought herself head over heels in love the last time and had been much too precipitate, given herself to Crispin too soon. So she had vowed to be careful in the future, to make her head rule her heart. But her head, unfortunately, couldn't keep her stupid heart from feeling excited and full of hope.

The rest of that day and most of the following two were spent mostly in Oliver's company, although Dyan made sure that Russ or some other member of the crew were often with them, or else she spent an hour or so alone in the ops room. She didn't want Oliver to think that she was monopolising him, although it was mainly the other way round; he sought her out. This was natural enough as he was a sort of guest on board and she was his host on the company's behalf, but she knew it was more than that. The smile he gave her, his eyes warm and interested, wasn't the same smile that he gave to anyone in the crew. And when she changed for dinner in the evenings into one of her new dresses, his appreciative glance told her a great deal.

But Dyan also had her reputation with the crew to consider and didn't want to get herself talked about, so she was circumspect and would often call Hal or someone over to join them as they sat out on the deck or in the rest-room after dinner.

Late in the afternoon of their third full day at sea, they motored quietly into the harbour at Antigua to pick up the other four members of the crew. But here they met the first snag of the voyage. One of the divers they were to pick up had been involved in an accident on the way to meet them. Dyan went ashore with Russ and Hal to visit him, but found that he wouldn't be fit to work for at least a month.

The three of them had a conference after they left the hospital.

'It could be a month before we find the boat we're looking for,' Hal pointed out. 'He could join us then.'

'Or we could find it straight off. We need a full complement of divers on this job. I'm going to call

Barney and have him fly someone else out to us,' Dyan said decisively.

'It will mean staying in Antigua for a couple of days,' Russ warned her.

'Well, that can't be helped. I'm not going to risk this lift without enough men.'

So, instead of immediately putting out to sea again, they found themselves having to wait at one of the most lively tourist resorts in the Caribbean.

'Will it be OK to let the guys go ashore tonight?' Russ asked her.

She nodded. 'I don't see why not. It will be some time before we're back on land again so they might as well make the most of the delay.'

Russ made the announcement to the men as soon as they got back to the ship. He gave them no warnings about keeping their mouths shut, or not getting drunk, because these were all well-paid, responsible men, who wanted to keep their jobs. He knew they could be relied on to enjoy themselves without getting into trouble. The men gave a cheer and went off to get ready to go ashore. Even the cook got the evening off.

Afterwards, Oliver came over to Dyan. 'Have you been to Antigua before?'

'Oh, yes, several times.'

'Then perhaps you know somewhere good where we can eat?' He gave her one of his slow smiles. 'That's if you'll have dinner with me, of course?'

Dyan felt her heart flutter a little, but she said off-handedly, 'Thanks. We may as well keep each other company, I suppose.'

An amused glint came into Oliver's eyes as he said smoothly, 'Of course.'

Dyan went to change, unable to stop the zing of excitement bubbling in her veins. She brushed her hair into a loose mane around her head, put on make-up, and a cream dress that accentuated her tan and clung in all the right places. Looking at herself critically in the mirror, Dyan saw that she was looking her best, and deliberately stifled mental reminders that she wasn't out to encourage Oliver. Well, tonight was time out; tomorrow she would be back to normal again.

Oliver was waiting for her in the rest-room, wearing a white dinner-jacket and dark trousers, smart but casual clothes. He turned round as she came in and his eyes widened very satisfactorily. 'You look—stunning,' he said as he let out his breath. Then he grinned. 'You ought to be a fashion model. No one in the world would ever think that you're in charge of ''this expedition, this ship and these men''.'

'Aren't you ever going to let me forget that?' she asked, laughing.

'Well, I certainly won't.' He paused and added teasingly, 'And one day maybe I'll tell you why.'

Intrigued, she immediately became terribly feminine, giving him a wide-eyed look. 'Tell me now,' she coaxed.

Taking her hand, Oliver laughed. 'Oh, no. Come on, let's go ashore.'

Dyan reported to Russ first, telling him where she could be found in case of emergency, noting that the three crewmen who had come aboard that day were standing watch.

They took a cab to a nightclub that served some of the best West Indian food in the Caribbean. It was an unusual place, with a straw roof and rows of tables in tiers above a dance-floor that looked too big for the room. A steel band played while the customers ate; music to dance to between courses. They had a couple of piña coladas served in tall glasses with fruit falling out the sides while Dyan described the dishes on the menu for Oliver. He made several witty, outrageous, comments about the dishes which made her laugh, and she suddenly felt intensely happy.

Oliver, too, seemed much more relaxed, and he deliberately set out to amuse and entertain her. She had thought him good company before, but here he seemed to come into his own, to be the kind of companion a girl dreamed about. And it became clear why when he leaned across the table after they'd given their order, and took her hand in his as he said, 'This is the first time I've ever really been alone with you. There are always so many other people around on board the ship.'

'Yes, I suppose there are,' Dyan agreed lightly, trying to decide whether or not to take her hand away.

'Mostly because you seem to invite people to join us,' Oliver said, watching her.

She didn't try to deny it, but said, 'Do you mind?'

'Yes. They cramp my style.'

Her eyes came up to meet his at that. 'Oh! Really?' she said in surprise, not quite knowing how to take it.

His mouth curved in amusement. It was a very sexy mouth, now she came to think about it. 'Really,' he assured her gravely.

She took her hand away. 'I suppose you've had plenty of practice, back in London,' she said on an offhand note.

'Ah.' Oliver leant back in his chair. 'I think we've reached the moment when you're supposed to say,

"But I know nothing about you".' He imitated a girlish voice, overdoing it, making her give a gurgle of laughter.

'Am I? I didn't realise we'd reached that moment.' The laughter was still in her eyes but there was a question in her voice.

'Oh, yes, I think so.' He gave her one of his laconic smiles. 'Now, where shall I begin? I'm thirty-two. Educated and civilised at a public school, knocked into shape and a career at university—Cambridge in my case. The only son of terribly respectable parents...' His voice was flippant, but now his eyes settled on her face. 'And I'm what you might call experienced, but definitely heart-free.'

Dyan smiled but looked away, thinking that she could probably say the same about herself. But it was different for a man; for him it was OK to be experienced, necessary almost, but what would a man—especially one with those terribly respectable parents—think of a woman who admitted she was experienced too? On the other hand, it was good to know that he was definitely unattached, and interesting that he wanted her to know.

She didn't speak and Oliver said, 'Aren't you going to reciprocate?'

'You already know all about me,' she said with a slight shrug.

'All about your work, yes. But I'm sure there's far more to you than that.'

For a moment she thought of telling him everything, but the impulse was quickly gone. It was too soon, and she didn't know him well enough. And, anyway, it was all in the past, dead and buried, so why the hell should she let it spoil the present? Tossing her head so that her hair swung around her shoulders, Dyan said pertly, 'You want another reference? I'll show you my CV if you'll show me yours.'

Oliver laughed delightedly. 'I might just do that.'

'But not tonight,' she said on a definite note. 'Do you know how to dance, Mr Insurance Man?'

'Before I could walk,' he assured her.

She wrinkled her nose at him. 'Well, are you going to ask me or are we going to sit here all night?'

Getting to his feet, Oliver said, 'Now do I give a formal bow and ask for the pleasure of this dance— or do I just say, "Let's shake it, babe"?'

'Wow, the two sides of Oliver Balfour. I didn't know you were a Jekyll-and-Hyde character.'

'Of course. I turn into a werewolf at midnight.'

'Oh, well; as long as it isn't into a frog.' And she stood up to join him.

Oliver laughed again, making people turn to look at them. He took her hand, his eyes alight with amusement, and led her on to the floor.

He hadn't been exaggerating when he'd said that he could dance; he was really good, swinging her into the rhythm, holding her firmly in his arms as they swung to the beat. 'Can you jive?' he asked her.

'You mean all that old-fashioned, out-of-date stuff that went out in the Sixties?'

'Watch it!'

She laughed. 'I'll give it a try.' Then gasped as he immediately began to jive, swinging her out, twisting her round, and catching her hand to send her swirling again. At the end she was dizzy and clung to Oliver for a moment, laughing up at him. 'Where did you learn to do that?' she exclaimed.

'I told you, at my mother's knee. She used to love dancing, but my father was away a lot, so she used to make me dance with her,' he told her as he led her back to their table.

'Doesn't she dance any more?'

'Oh, yes; my father has retired now and they go to lots of tea-dances as well as evening dances. And she insists that I always go with them whenever I'm home.'

'Do they still jive?'

'Yes, of course.'

'She certainly taught you well,' Dyan told him, thinking that any middle-aged lady and gentleman who could still jive like that couldn't be as ultra-respectable and stuffy as Oliver had made them sound.

'Thank you, ma'am.' Oliver bowed his head at the compliment. 'Would you like another one of these concoctions?' he asked, gesturing at her glass.

She shook her head. 'I'll wait for the wine.'

It soon came with their first course, bongo bongo soup, one of the specialities of the house, and made with fresh oysters. The legend about oysters being an aphrodisiac crossed Dyan's mind, but she didn't say anything. Although, judging from the amusement in Oliver's eyes, his own thoughts weren't a million miles away from hers.

They didn't dance again until their meal was finished, instead talking of their likes and dislikes in sport, the theatre, films, that kind of thing, feeling their way, getting to know one another.

Dyan looked at Oliver over the rim of her glass as she drank, watching as he eloquently told her some anecdote, liking what she saw more and more. He seemed to be very self-assured, very confident. He had travelled a lot, could talk about skiing in Zermatt, ballooning in Africa. He had done things she'd never attempted, but his descriptions of them made her long to try; he'd been to places that his descriptions now made her ache to see. His eloquence opened up a new world to her, which was what a good conversation-alist was supposed to do, she realised. Converse, convert; no wonder the two words were so alike in their root.

He didn't say anything about any women in his past, though; that experience he'd claimed to have was still a closed book, but Dyan had no doubt whatsoever that he was a man of the world in that aspect, too. But she had yet to discover how broad-minded he was. And that thought troubled her because he had been so chauvinistic at first about her job. Not that he was now; quite the reverse; he seemed to have accepted her competence completely. And it had pleased her a lot that he hadn't called Barney.

They danced once more before the floor show came on; a colourful, agile group of native dancers came on first, drums beating, skirts swaying as they leapt athletically around the floor, the sweat of perspir-ation on their dark, glistening limbs. They were fol-lowed by fire-eaters, Dyan's face unknowingly cringing as she watched, until Oliver leaned forward and whis-pered, 'They probably practise on that Creole chicken we had,' which made her quickly cover her mouth to stop the laughter from bursting out.

Then the spotlights centred on a limbo dancer, who looked much too tall to possibly get under the low bar, less than a foot from the ground. But he was thin and lithe, had fantastic balance as he sank lower and lower and crept inch by inch under it as the audience held their breath, then burst into applause as he made it and jumped quickly to his feet. Then he did the whole thing again with the bar on fire this time!

After the applause had again died down, the lights dimmed, only the candles in low pots on the tables lighting the room. Tacitly, everyone became very quiet. A man began to sing, his voice soft then slowly rising; old, old songs that told of the longing of black slaves for their homeland in Africa, melodies that were haunting and sad. He had the most beautiful voice that caught at your heart, made you feel the despair and suffering. Her heart wrung, Dyan's hand clenched as it lay on the table, but Oliver's reached out to cover it. She turned to look at him in the semi-darkness, knowing that he understood, that he wanted to comfort her. His eyes held hers steadily, and after a moment she turned her hand and let him take hers.

CHAPTER THREE

WHEN the long, plaintive note of his last song had died completely away, the lights gradually brightened. The audience gave a collective sigh, blinking back to the present. Dyan removed her hand, a slight flush on her cheeks, and joined in the great burst of appreciative applause. But it was cut short as the dancers came bounding back on to the floor, all of them wearing colourful feather skirts and nothing else, the women, too. The dancers ran among the audience, shaking madly to the beat in front of one table then another. One, a young girl with full, uptilted breasts, noticed Oliver and came to stand right in front of him as she jiggled and shook. Dyan glanced at him curiously, but he watched the girl, not embarrassed, not leering, just amused appreciation in his face.

The dancer, pouting, ran back on the floor to join the others; they performed their last, amazingly energetic number, and then left the stage empty for general dancing again. Once more the lights dimmed as the band played a slow love theme.

Oliver reached out for her hand. 'Shall we?'

His arm went round her, holding Dyan close against him, her hands resting lightly on his shoulders. There were a lot of American tourists in the club, the men wearing white dinner-jackets like Oliver's, most of them tall, some of them good-looking men. But there was something about Oliver that made him stand out from the rest. At first she thought it was his English-

ness, his innate reserve in comparison to the more ex-
pansive Americans. But it wasn't entirely that, and
for several minutes Dyan couldn't pin down the quality
she was looking for. Then it came to her: the other
men were being over-masculine, flaunting it almost,
as if to prove their virility, but Oliver wasn't like that,
for the simple reason that he had nothing to prove to
anyone, let alone a roomful of strangers. He was su-
premely self-confident and complete in himself. In the
job she had, Dyan had met a lot of tough men who
had proved their worth and earned the respect of their
fellows, but she had never met a man who seemed so
innately masculine as Oliver, who appeared sure of
himself in every aspect of his character, and to have
had that quality all his life.

The thought excited her, but made her cautious,
too. Every girl had a dream man, whether they denied
it or not. Most of the time the dream man remained
a dream and the girls would settle, happily enough,
for prosaic reality. Or perhaps what they had thought
to be their dream man would become just an ordinary
man like the next guy, after all. That had happened
to Dyan and now made her doubly cautious, especially as her dream man had turned out to be a liar
and a cheat. But Oliver? Oliver was becoming
dreamier by the minute—and that could be dangerous.

That thought made her move a little away from him.
'The dancers were amazing, weren't they?' she remarked, wanting to lighten the mood.

'Amazing,' Oliver agreed, and tightened his arm to
draw her back against him.

Dyan gave a small smile, thinking, Oh, well, I tried,
and let herself relax, her body against his as they
danced. She found that it was a very exciting place

to be. Dyan was fully aware of him, of his height and the breadth of his shoulders, of his clean-cut features and his mouth that seemed to have the beginnings of a lazy smile at its corners. Now and again their legs would brush, and she had to concentrate hard to control the quiver that it sent through her. This won't do, she told herself; this is too much, too soon. But what was it really except two colleagues having a night off to dine and dance together?

But it was developing into more than that; she knew it and so did Oliver. He smiled down at her, a warm look that sent a surge of anticipation coursing through her. He took one of her hands in his and brushed it lightly with his lips, so lightly that it couldn't be called a kiss, so lightly that she could even have been mistaken. But his eyes were holding hers, watching her, and she knew that their relationship had taken another small step along its way.

They had another drink, danced a few more times when the music was slow. They didn't talk much as they danced, were content just to be close. After an hour or so, Oliver leaned across the table and took her hand. 'Shall we go?'

She nodded, and went to the cloakroom while he settled the bill. Looking at herself in the mirror, Dyan noticed that her eyes seemed strangely extra wide, that excitement played in their green depths. I must control this, she thought. I don't want to be hurt again. But it was difficult to be cool when your heart was singing and your pulse racing. She felt like a teenager on her first date, not a sophisticated woman of twenty-six, and chided herself for it. I'll be totally in control, she ordered herself, as she renewed and blotted her lipstick. I'll be my age and not let him see that I like him.

This determined resolve held for the whole of two minutes, until Dyan walked out to join Oliver and found him standing waiting for her. He was leaning nonchalantly against the wall, his hands in his trouser pockets, his hard profile outlined against the soft glow of a lamp. He turned, saw her, straightened up, and smiled. It was the smile that did it, warm, almost like a caress. Dyan's heart gave a great kick in her chest and she knew that she was falling in love all over again.

When they got outside, Oliver drew her arm through his. 'Is the sea far from here?'

'No.' She pointed. 'About half a mile away.'

'Is there a beach?'

She nodded, realising why he was asking, and said huskily, 'Yes, there's a beach.'

'Let's take a walk there, then.'

She hesitated for only a moment before falling into step beside him.

It was a beautiful night, the moon soft and golden in the sky, the air heavy with the scent of the thousands of tropical plants that grew wild on the island. They passed a grove of hibiscus, their flowers a lovely gift to the world for a day but closed and faded now with nightfall. But there was bougainvillaea everywhere, hanging from old wrought-iron balconies, tumbling over walls, the crimson and purple flowers like flame in the lamplight.

The sound of the sea grew nearer, the houses fewer, until they reached the long, snaking shoreline, the white sand silver in the moonlight.

'Are you OK to walk on the sand?' Oliver asked.

Dyan held his arm and bent to take off her high-heeled sandals. 'Now I am.'

There was a breeze but it was off the land and was warm, and carried with it the sound of music from one of the open-air bars, its beat soft and sensuous. Out to sea they could see the lights of fishing boats bobbing with the waves. There were other people around, strolling along like themselves, or sitting in groups under the swaying palm trees over a fire of coconut husks that set sparks shooting up into the darkness. But the atmosphere was peaceful, languorous; there were no rowdy parties or drunks to spoil the beauty and tranquillity of the night.

'This is a great place,' Oliver remarked. 'I like it here.'

'You must come for a holiday some time,' Dyan said lightly. 'The water sports are terrific.'

'How long have we got before your replacement diver arrives?'

'He's due in late tomorrow afternoon.'

'Then how about making tomorrow a holiday, try out some of the water sports? That's unless you have to be on the ship,' he added.

'No. I'm free, I guess.'

'Good.' He drew her arm closer through his and held her hand as they walked further along the beach. There were fewer people around as they left the town behind, those they passed were mostly couples, their arms around each other, with no attention to spare for anyone but themselves. Others were sitting on the sand, close in each other's embrace.

'This is a popular honeymoon resort,' Dyan felt compelled to explain.

Oliver laughed. 'I thought it must be something in the air.' And added, 'I was hoping it was catching.'

Dyan had nothing to say to that. They walked on, passed a group of young people, skinny-dipping in the shallows.

'The joys of youth,' Oliver remarked with a grin.

'You're not old.'

'I'm too old for that kind of party,' he said firmly.

I wonder if I am? Dyan thought. She'd spent so much time single-mindedly working on her career, and then waiting around for Crispin to show up, that she seemed to have lost a lot of her youth. Not that it usually worried her very much, except at odd moments like this when she realised that she was no longer in those first, glorious and absolutely carefree years of youth and freedom from responsibility. But would she still go skinny-dipping? Not in a group, certainly. But alone? Or with just one other person? With a man? Which man, wasn't difficult to imagine. And the thought of Oliver naked excited her. Beneath his well-cut clothes he must have a beautiful body. She wondered what he would be like as a lover, and thought that it had been a very long time since she had been physically loved.

They left the swimmers and everyone else behind, came to a palm tree that had fallen across the sand and barred the way. Oliver stepped over it and turned to help Dyan. She stepped up on to the trunk and went to jump off it when Oliver saw her face in the moonlight, eyes heavy and her lips parted sensuously.

'What are you thinking?' he demanded.

'What?' The question took her by surprise. She lost her balance, swayed.

But Oliver reached swiftly out and caught her, lifted her down on to the sand. His hands were on her waist and he left them there as he looked down at her, deep into her eyes as if striving to read her errant, wanton thoughts. 'Dyan.' He said her name softly, almost on a note of discovery.

She didn't speak, just stood gazing up at his face, made hard and angular in the moonlight. A great feeling of breathless anticipation filled her, as if this was a moment that she had waited for a very long time, and she must do nothing, not speak, not move, or it would fade away.

So when Oliver bent his head to take her lips he found them unresisting. He kissed her lightly at first, but firmly for all that; there was nothing tentative about it. Rather, he explored her mouth, taking his time, as if savouring every millionth of a second, tasting the soft, tremulous fullness of her lips, letting the languor of the caress match the languor of the night.

Dyan let out her breath in a long sigh, a sound that came from the depth of her heart. Without realising it, she lifted her arms to rest her hands on his shoulders. The movement, slight though it was, brushed her body against his. Oliver's hands tightened on her waist; he began to rain little kisses that plucked her lips insidiously, made her want to respond, but his lips had moved on again before she could. She began to feel a great ache of awareness, of frustrated need; a sensation that started deep down inside her, and one that she hadn't experienced for a very long time. Involuntarily she moved nearer to him, so that their bodies were close all the way down, and her hands went up around his neck.

Oliver made a small sound deep in his throat. Of satisfaction? Perhaps of need. The languor was completely gone as his shoulders hunched and now, at last, he took her mouth fully. Almost instantly her senses began to swirl, and Dyan clung to him, lost in a giddy whirlpool of desire. The shock of it, the immediate blitz on her emotions, made her heart almost stop beating. It seemed as if she was suspended in time, in motion, helpless beneath the searing sensuality of his kiss. His embrace deepened, became passionate, and her mouth opened under the onslaught. She moaned, her breath coming now in short, shuddering gasps as she began to drown in the wonder of it.

'Dyan! Dyan!' Oliver's voice was thick, unsteady. His mouth left hers as his lips caressed her throat, her shoulders, driving her mad. But then he pulled her hard against him, letting her know that he was aroused, as he took her lips again in fierce, urgent hunger.

The hardness of his body evoked an even greater need in her own. Putting her hands in his hair, she pulled herself against him, gave an aching cry of desire. Oliver's hand went to her breast, his fingers through the thin silk of her dress setting every nerve-end on fire, erotic, sensual. Her nipple hardened as he caressed it and she gave a gasping moan of exquisite, aching desire. Hearing, recognising it, he let his hand slide slowly along her quivering body, down to her waist and hip, across the flat plane of her stomach to her thigh. His kisses became compulsive, then—and he began to lower her towards the soft, silver bed of the sand.

But for Dyan it was suddenly too much; the invasion of her senses, the great tide of sexuality, overwhelmed her, and with a small cry she pushed him away and broke free.

Oliver immediately reached for her again, but she said, 'No!' sharply.

He stood beside her, his breathing uneven, and for the first time since she'd known him he seemed to momentarily have lost his self-possession. 'What's the matter?' he got out, his voice ragged.

'You—you're going too fast for me.'

Lifting a hand, Oliver pushed back a lock of hair that had fallen on his forehead, and got his breath under control. 'We're both adults,' he pointed out.

'Not that adult, I'm not,' Dyan said firmly.

That made him laugh, which at once eased the tension. 'Sorry. I—er—thought we were getting along rather well.'

'Not well enough for that,' Dyan said a little breathlessly. Though why she said it she didn't know, because they had definitely been getting on very well indeed. But the crazy surge of feelings had frightened her; never before had she been so completely oblivious to anything else but the forcefulness of sexual desire, the overwhelming urge to fulfil it.

'No?' Oliver came to stand in front of her. He put his hands on her arms, caressed them gently, so that she felt no alarm. But then he answered his own question. 'No, of course not. I'm afraid I got rather carried away.' He laughed, half ruefully, half in surprise. 'That hasn't happened to me for a very long time.'

'It must be the moonlight,' she said lightly.

He shook his head and said with certainty, 'No, not the moonlight. You know that. I'm very, very attracted to you, Dyan.' Bending, he lightly kissed her eyelids, her cheek, her lips. When she slowly opened her eyes, he was looking down at her, his gaze intent. 'I don't remember ever having experienced anything quite like this before,' he murmured on a note of wonder.

'This?' She badly wanted to know what he meant, but was strangely afraid again, so she said teasingly, 'You mean—having the girl say no?'

Oliver laughed and lifted a finger to lightly tap her nose in admonition. 'No, that is not what I meant.'

'Oh?' She gave him a pert look. 'So you mean they always say yes.'

He gave a growl, put his arms round her, and hugged her to him, like a big bear. 'Here am I trying to be serious and you keep teasing me, woman,' he complained.

Getting an arm free, Dyan lifted her hand and ran her fingertips over his mouth. 'We hardly know each other,' she said softly, excuse in her tone. 'We only met a few days ago.'

'Long enough to know that we like each other. Long enough to recognise the sexual attraction that we both feel. And don't say that it isn't there,' Oliver added, capturing her hand. 'You know it as well as I do.'

'I wasn't going to deny it,' Dyan admitted. 'But...' She paused, seeking the right words, but Oliver finished the sentence for her.

'But you're not the kind of girl who goes with a man on the first date.'

'I'm not the kind of girl who goes with a man after a *dozen* dates,' Dyan admitted, making him grin. 'I missed out on the sexual emancipation generation. I'm afraid that tonight has given you the wrong idea of me.'

Oliver gave a small frown. 'You're not saying that . . .'

Guessing what he meant, Dyan blushed, and said, 'No, I'm not saying that. I'm not completely inexperienced. But maybe tonight I got carried away, too.' She looked up at him, wanting him to understand. But, still not wanting to get serious, she gave him a mock punch in the chest and said in a strong American accent, 'You darned swept me off my feet back there, buster!'

He smiled but his eyes were serious as he said, 'And I, too, got a lot more than I bargained for.' He looked at her, but when she didn't speak, he said, 'So—we take it slowly?'

'Yes, please.'

Taking her hand, Oliver turned it over and kissed the palm, his lips sensuous, making her suddenly want him desperately. Her hand, her whole body quivered with awareness. Feeling it, Oliver's grip tightened and he gave her a look in which her own naked need was mirrored. 'But it's going to happen,' he said on a harsh note. 'You know that.'

Dyan tried to speak but couldn't, could only stare at him, not wanting to commit herself, but knowing in her heart that he was right.

With a sudden movement, Oliver took her in his arms again and held her tightly against him. 'I want you, Dyan,' he said, his voice hoarse with desire. 'Oh, don't worry, I'm not going to coerce you. But when you do say yes I hope it will be on a night like this, with moonlight and palm trees and the sound of the sea.'

She smiled tenderly and put up a hand to gently stroke his cheek. 'I wouldn't have it any other way,' she assured him.

Looking down at her, Oliver gave a small laugh. 'Lord, what a night. One to remember. How long have we got on this voyage?'

'A month at least, maybe a couple of weeks more.'

'Couldn't you contrive not to find the wreck so that we have longer?'

She gave a gurgle of laughter. 'If your bosses could only hear you now!'

'Who gives a damn about them?' He took the lobe of her ear in his mouth and gently bit it. 'Don't keep me waiting too long, my darling; I don't know how long I'm going to be able to control myself when I'm near you every day.'

Dyan gazed up at him, her eyes searching his face. She wanted to tell him that she felt the same, that the overwhelming attraction she felt for him went even deeper, that she was falling in love with him. But she was too scared, too afraid that this might not be the real thing after all. It had all happened too quickly— just as it had with Crispin—and her mind was full of doubts. She wanted to commit herself, to let the excitement and happiness that surged within her take over her mind as well as her heart, but fear of being hurt again held her back. So instead of saying anything she merely reached up and kissed him, then, before he could reciprocate, drew back and said, 'We'd better get back to the ship.'

'Will they send out a search party?'

'No, but I don't want the crew to—gossip about us.'

'I see.' There was a note of disappointment in his tone, but he helped her over the fallen palm and walked beside her along the beach. 'Is that what you're afraid of: losing your reputation with the crew, with Starr Marine?'

Dyan shook her head. 'No. My private life is my own. But I'd rather the men didn't make assumptions about us, talk about us, until—well, until I'm ready to commit—I mean, if I'm ever ready to—to...'

She couldn't finish and Oliver burst into laughter. 'Say when, not if, my darling.' His dark eyes held hers. 'Because we are definitely going to become lovers, and I hope very soon.'

Licking lips gone dry, Dyan said, 'I thought you said you weren't going to coerce me.'

He raised an eyebrow. 'Would you call that coercion?'

'Definitely.'

He grinned and put his arm round her waist as they strolled along. 'You will still spend tomorrow with me, won't you?' Oliver asked on a suddenly anxious note.

'Yes, of course.'

'Great. There are going to be so few opportunities to be alone with you once we're back at sea.'

They fell silent, but it was a close, comfortable silence, each aware of the other's thoughts, thinking of what had passed that night and looking forward to the next day.

When they reached the town it was Oliver who led her back through the streets so that they emerged on to the dock as if they'd come from the town, not the beach, and she was pleased by his tact. The man on watch greeted them and they said goodnight within his hearing, Dyan thanking Oliver for a pleasant evening and he politely thanking her in turn for her company, but unable to keep a flash of devilment out of his eyes.

They parted then, Dyan going below to her cabin, but not to sleep. She was overwhelmingly glad and relieved that she had managed to say no to him. Now they would be able to take this new romance slowly, find out if this attraction that had overwhelmed them both was just desire or something more. Dyan was pretty sure of her own feelings, not that she trusted them, but not at all sure about Oliver's. Maybe he didn't even know himself, although he had said that nothing like this had happened to him before. But it was all too soon, too quick; just like the last time. And look how that had turned out! With a feeling of great bitterness Dyan blamed her old love for spoiling this new romance. How could she possibly relax and enjoy being in love again when all the time the shadow of doubt that Crispin had put in her mind hung over her? She had vowed then never to trust a man again, and that promise wasn't easy to cast aside.

A dozen times she told herself that Oliver was far different, that she shouldn't judge one man by the other. But Crispin, too, had swept her off her feet, making her feel that she was in love, and had tried to take her to bed at once, just as Oliver had tried to do. But there the similarity ends, she told herself. Oliver isn't married. But Crispin had told her that, too, and it had turned out to be a lie. Maybe it would be as well to check on Oliver, although the thought of doing so was infinitely distasteful. Reluctantly,

Dyan decided to do so as soon as possible, so that she could be sure of that at least. But in the meantime, she had tomorrow to look forward to, and Dyan fell asleep at last with a soft smile on her lips.

Oliver had evidently accepted her ground rules; when she walked into the galley the next morning he greeted her casually, and asked if he could use the phone. As Dyan had just been using it to check on him this brought a slight colour to her cheeks, but she hoped he hadn't noticed, or had put it down to embarrassment. She gave permission and helped herself to breakfast as he went to the office.

Not wanting to get any ribald comments from Barney Starr, Dyan had spoken to his secretary, a woman she knew she could trust, who had promised to make the necessary enquiries and let her know as soon as possible. But Dyan didn't expect to hear for at least a couple of days, and so determinedly pushed it out of her mind. After breakfast, when most of the crew had gone ashore again, she went back to her cabin and changed into a new bikini with a matching skirt and top, the skirt slit up to the top of her leg, and the loose shirt tied in a knot at the front, leaving her midriff bare. Her hair she plaited into one long braid that lay heavy down her back. Maybe she would untie it later, but if they swam it was better this way. And it didn't look too sexy. Although whether that was for the crew's or Oliver's benefit, Dyan wasn't at all sure.

She stuffed a towel into her bag and went up on deck, her sunspecs perched on her head as usual. Oliver wasn't around and someone said he had gone ashore, so she went to talk to Russ on the bridge.

'I've checked with London,' she told him. 'The new diver caught his flight to Miami OK. The connecting flight should get here around four-thirty, and I've arranged for Hal to go and pick him up. We'll sail as soon as we can after he arrives.'

'OK, boss,' he replied laconically.

Glancing down at the dock, Dyan saw Oliver drive up in a big American convertible, the hood down. Getting out of the car, he looked up at the ship, saw her and waved, compelling her to add, 'Er—I promised Oliver I'd show him something of the island.'

Russ glanced at her, saw the over-casual look on her face, and he grinned, his eyebrows rising. 'Sure.'

Dyan could have killed him, but knew he wouldn't make any remarks to the rest of the crew. 'He hasn't been here before,' she said in useless justification. 'And I'll be back in plenty of time.'

'Better get going, then. You don't want to keep the client waiting.'

She shot him a look, but went ashore eagerly enough.

'I managed to hire a car,' Oliver said with a grin, his eyes lingering on her, the attraction he felt unsuppressed. 'If you can call it a car; it feels like I'm driving a tank. And although everyone drives on the left-hand side of the road, all the cars have steering-wheels on the wrong side.'

'You'll soon get used to it.'

Dyan got in beside him, but before they drove away Oliver leaned nearer and shaking his head, complained, 'I do wish you wouldn't do it.'

She gave him a startled look. 'Do what?'

'Look more beautiful every time I see you. If I eventually lose control of myself, my darling, it will be entirely your own fault.'

'Oh, that's a good one,' she said appreciatively. 'Blaming it on the girl in advance, in case the guy gets randy.'

His brows drew together in a pained look. 'Randy! What a word.'

'Isn't it what you would say?'

Oliver shook his head, his eyes caressing. 'It certainly doesn't describe the way I feel about you.'

Dyan caught her breath, wanting to say that she felt the same way, but then common sense came to her aid; it was too early in the day for such intensity. So she merely smiled and said, 'Where are we going?'

Tacitly accepting her decision, Oliver patted the steering-wheel. 'The island is our oyster with this thing. How about just driving until we run out of road?'

'Sounds good.'

They drove up through the port and into the town of St John's, the capital of the island, through its busy, colourful streets, where every shop seemed to find it necessary to display half its goods outside on the pavement, pushing the straw-hatted pedestrians into the roadway.

'Do you know much about the island?' Oliver asked as he carefully threaded his way through the throng, the horn sounding to move a donkey that seemed to have gone on strike.

'Not a lot. I know that it's an independent state of the British Commonwealth, and that its chief export is rum, but that's about it. I could tell you a whole lot about the sea around it, though.'

Oliver laughed and accelerated a little as they left the busiest streets of the town behind. 'You can tell me all about that when we get to sea, on one of the days—which I'm afraid are going to be terribly long and frustrating—when the crew will be around and all I'll be able to do is look at you.'

They drove around for a while until the road Oliver had chosen eventually ran out at another beach, at some distance from the town, with only a couple of village type hotels spaced along the shore. The beach, though, was busy with holidaymakers, some sunbathing, others windsurfing, diving or, further out, waterskiing.

'What would you like to do first?'

'Ski,' Dyan replied promptly.

'Better leave our things locked in the car for now, then,' Oliver suggested.

Getting out, they took off their outer clothes. Oliver was wearing dark blue bathing shorts, and she had been right about his body: it was strong and lithe, smooth and athletic. Glancing at him, Dyan felt a great urge to run her hands over his chest, and had to quickly drop her head in case he should notice.

He had, of course; she might have known. Giving her an amused glance, Oliver put his hand under her chin and tilted her head so that she had to look at him. 'Thanks for the compliment,' he said with a grin.

'Compliment?' She opened her eyes wide in mock innocence.

He gave her a small kiss, then stood back and deliberately let his eyes travel slowly down her body. Then he looked at her and Dyan knew that the sexual awareness she saw in his eyes had been in her own. With a small laugh, she stopped pretending and dropped him a bobbing curtsy, 'And thank *you*, sir,' she said pertly.

Laughing, he put his hands on her waist, lifted her and spun her round. Then, still holding her above him, kissed her again.

Dyan returned the kiss, marvelling at his strength, and let her hands slide down his chest as he set her on her feet again. He made a groaning noise in his throat and shook his head in frustration. 'Let's go and swim first; I definitely need to get into some cold water!'

So they swam for a while, both of them good swimmers, then hired skis and a boat with a driver and spent about an hour on the water. Oliver said it had been a long time since he had waterskied and Dyan was better than he, but he soon got back into it after he'd fallen in a couple of times. They had fun, weaving by ducking under each other's rope, and once standing on the same skis, Oliver with his arms round her as they dashed along through the spray. That was good. The best.

'Why doesn't the driver take us further out?' Oliver asked once, between rides. 'He keeps turning to come back.'

'Sharks,' Dyan told him. 'We can't go out beyond the reef.'

'Of course. I'd forgotten.'

When their hour was up, they went to a palm-leaf thatched beach bar for a rum-punch, then sat on the beach in the shade of a palm tree to drink it. Oliver leaned against the trunk of the tree and Dyan leaned against him, his free arm round her waist.

'Where would you like to have lunch?' he asked, leaning forward to kiss her shoulder, his lips cool from the iced drink.

She gave a small shrug. 'Here. Anywhere. It doesn't matter.' She could have added, so long as it's with you, but didn't have to; when she looked over her shoulder at him, he read it in her eyes.

Oliver drew in a breath, then said on a long note of discovery, 'I've read the expression "drowning in a woman's eyes", but I've always thought it a very stupid and hackneyed phrase. But your eyes, they're such a deep, beautiful green. And so expressive. A man could easily——' He broke off, gave a rueful smile. 'But you must get tired of being told how beautiful you are. I expect every man you meet——'

'Don't be silly,' Dyan said softly. Turning, she put down her drink and placed her hands on either side of Oliver's face, so that she, too, could look into his eyes. But at first she didn't speak.

'What do you see?' Oliver asked in a mock-frightened voice.

'Your eyes are like the sea,' she said on a note of pleased discovery. 'They change colour—or seem to. When we first met they were pale grey, like the sea in winter, but now...'

'But now?' he prompted, deliberately letting them darken with desire.

She gave a small gurgle of laughter. 'But now they're warm and intent, like the waters of the gulf stream.'

'In a hurry to get where they're going,' Oliver put in, but with a different meaning.

She gave him a playful slap on the cheek. 'Naughty!' But then she frowned a little.

'What is it?'

Slowly, Dyan said, 'I think that your eyes have another mood, another colour. I think they can be dark and turbulent, when you're angry, like the sea when it's boiling up for a great storm.'

'Well, that isn't a colour you're likely to see, my lovely one.' Oliver bent to brush her lips with his, small, insistent kisses that made them both wish they were alone. When they drew back he smiled and said, 'Did you know that there are tiny golden flecks in your eyes?' She shook her head. 'And did you know that I find you incredibly, overwhelmingly beautiful?'

This time he kissed her properly, his arms round her as they leaned against the tree. It was the right sort of kiss: deeply satisfying for the moment, but wanting more as soon as their lips parted.

It was several minutes before either of them became aware of their surroundings again, before either of them spoke, but then Oliver gave a rueful smile and said, 'I'm sorry, I've an idea I'm behaving like a teenager who's just discovered—well, who's made quite a startling discovery.' Getting to his feet, he pulled her up beside him. 'Come on, temptress, let's go and have something to eat.'

When they'd eaten they walked along to the far end of the beach and hired a couple of jet-skis for half an hour, racing each other, and both ending up in the water when Dyan took a bend too fast. She came off with a shriek, but next moment found that Oliver had abandoned his machine and jumped in after her.

'Are you OK?'

She smiled at him, wiping the water from her eyes. 'Yes. Fine.' But she'd liked the note of anxiety in his voice.

They swam to the beach and walked back to their patch of shade. Oliver took her hand, twining his fingers through hers, and their shoulders were close. They walked slowly, hardly looking where they were going, often gazing into each other's eyes. Like lovers, Dyan thought. Only we're not—not yet. A *frisson* of sexual anticipation, achingly deep, ran through her, and she knew she would always remember this moment as they walked hand in hand along the shore, the sky a cloudless blue overhead, and the palm trees casting dancing shadows on the white sand.

The sun had moved round and their towels were no longer in the shade. Oliver knelt to shake them out and move them, while Dyan reached up to undo her plait, which was wet and heavy. She stood in the sun as she shook out her hair, freeing it from the braid. Glancing up, Oliver saw her and caught his breath, becoming still as he watched. For a few moments Dyan wasn't aware of him; she stood with her head tilted towards the sun, eyes closed, the rich chestnut of her hair turned to a living flame, her body tall and slender and golden, like a statue. But what was most enthralling was the absolute naturalness of her actions, her unawareness of the stunning picture of youth and beauty that she made. It wasn't until she'd shaken her hair free and it stood out in a thick halo of curls around her head, that Dyan glanced down at Oliver and found him staring up at her, almost in an attitude of worship, a punch-drunk kind of look on his face.

She raised her brows. 'What is it?'

He blinked and shook his head, gave a small laugh. Then reached up a hand and pulled her down beside him. 'Come here,' he said huskily.

They lay down on the towels together, their limbs warm from the sun, the sexual tension between them very strong. Oliver kissed her, his hand firm on her waist, and it was all he could do to keep from stroking her, to stop his hand from roaming where it shouldn't. Gritting his teeth, he gave a groan of frustration, and Dyan knew that if they had been alone he would have taken her—and she wouldn't have been able to resist him.

As it was, they lay close, kissed several times, talked, laughed a little, enjoying their few precious hours together. Oliver went in for another swim, but Dyan stayed on the beach, watching. He was a fast, powerful swimmer. But then, she thought, he's powerful in every way: in physical strength, mental ability, the force of his personality—and his ability to arouse her sexually; this last on a breath of nervous excitement. If they'd been staying in Antigua for another night... And then thought, *if only* they'd been staying in Antigua for another night!

When Oliver came out of the water it was time to get back to the ship. He dried himself and they walked reluctantly back to the car, but as they neared it, Dyan said, 'Oh, look! An autograph tree.'

'A what?'

She drew him to the low tree with its white flowers and thick, large leaves. 'See, you can write your name on the leaves, like this,' and she pointed to some of the leaves with names and messages already carved on them. 'The conquistadors are supposed to have used them for writing-paper.'

'Well, what's good enough for them must be good enough for us. Wait a moment.' He went to the car and came back with a penknife. 'Now, let's find a really good big one. Yes, I think this one will do. Turn around,' he commanded her.

Obediently, she did so, and didn't try to peep until Oliver told her she could look. He held the leaf out for her to see. In its thick green softness he had written his own name, then a heart, the symbol of love, and then her name. 'Oliver loves Dyan.'

'There,' he said huskily. 'Now everyone knows.'

CHAPTER FOUR

THE next three weeks were the most frustrating, but perhaps the most tensely exciting, that Dyan had ever known. After they left Antigua, it took only just over a day of steady sailing to reach the point off the Lesser Antilles which was the last known position of the *Xanadu*. Most of that day Dyan spent at her desk in the ops room, using weather charts that plotted the course of the hurricane that had hit and sunk the smaller ship, along with the *Xanadu's* log which the captain had managed to save, and his account of the time they left Barbados, their speed, and the time the hurricane had hit them. With all these facts, she was able to work out the area they must search. But in the evening, out of courtesy, she showed her figures to Russ, who checked them over with her and, as usual, had no fault to find.

'I don't know why you bothered to show these to me, Logan,' he remarked in his usual downright manner. 'Waste of time. Next time, just tell me where we're going.'

'OK, Skipper. Thanks.' She nodded, pleased, because this was Russ's way of saying that he trusted her, a great compliment.

Because she was working so hard, Dyan only saw Oliver at dinner that night, when all the crew who weren't on watch were also there, so they had no chance to talk. And the next day they began their search for the wreck, although Oliver made a point of coming up to her on deck to find out exactly why they were sailing up and down in parallel lines all the time.

'It's so that the sonar can do a trace of the sea-bottom,' Dyan explained. 'I thought I told you about that.'

'Did you? Something must have driven it out of my mind,' Oliver remarked, his eyes holding hers, laughter—and something much more important—in their grey depths.

So, for the benefit of those members of the crew who were standing within earshot, she explained again, gesturing out to sea, while Oliver said in her ear, 'Yesterday was one of the longest in my life. Did you deliberately hide yourself away?' Her eyes met his and he smiled, reading her answer. 'I nearly came looking for you a dozen times. And if this is how I feel after only one day without you, by the time this voyage is over I shall be smashing down the door of the ops room to get to you.' Leaning closer, he murmured, 'So don't say you haven't been warned, you siren.'

Unable to resist, Dyan said, 'Sirens lure men to their doom.'

Giving her a mock-leering look, Oliver said, 'Any time, honey. Any time. Just sing out and I'll be there.'

Which made Dyan burst out laughing, so that the men turned to look at them anyway.

Their days fell into the same pattern as the course they sailed over the water: one the same as the next, long, hot, and largely empty. Most of the crew developed their suntans, played cards, took French and Spanish lessons from a couple of men who were proficient in the languages. In the evenings they watched videos on television or made their own amusements. But these were intelligent men; several of them were taking Open University courses or working on some kind of project. One of the younger members of the crew wanted to be an oceanographer and, in the evenings, would get hold of Dyan so he could ask questions or get her to read his latest piece of work.

Usually she would have been pleased to help and encourage him, but she longed to be up on deck, because there, in the darkness of night, was the only place where she and Oliver could meet with any hope of being alone. Several times, in the deep shadow of the life-rafts, they had managed to sneak a little time together. Oliver would go up first and grab her as she walked by, apparently 'taking a last look round'. He would kiss her, then, hungrily, not letting her draw breath, kiss her until it was difficult for them both to control the gasps of desire, the panting sighs of passion. Dyan would cling to him as he put his hands low on her hips, holding her close against him, torturing them both.

He whispered words of love and need, told her how much he wanted her, how beautiful he found her. His hand would go to caress her breast, only to be removed with a groan, because it would have been too much, too exciting to bear. 'Sweetheart,' he murmured against her mouth. 'My darling, darling girl. I want you so much. God, how I want you!'

'I know. I know,' she breathed, her head thrown back as he kissed her throat, his hand in her hair, holding her still.

As the days went by it became harder, the sexual tension stronger. Dyan could only guess at what it was doing to Oliver, but it was driving her so mad

that she could think of little else. Once, they were up
on deck, decorously sitting next to each other in the
deckchairs, playing a game of chess. Oliver moved a
piece and Dyan frowned. 'The knight doesn't move
like that.' Glancing up, she saw Oliver looking at her,
with such deep, naked desire in his eyes, that she
gasped aloud.

'If you don't get this boat to shore soon,' he said
forcefully, 'I'll sink her so that we have to take to the
lifeboats.'

Another time she would have laughed, but not then,
because he spoke with such intensity.

But even though it was so frustrating, Dyan was
also overwhelmingly happy during those weeks. She
was sure, now, that she was in love, and in love for
keeps. And as the days passed the uncertainties and
distrust that her earlier, unhappy affair had sown,
faded away until she could look back on them almost
with disbelief, could laugh at how stupid she had been
to have any doubts about Oliver. When Barney's secretary sent her a fax which said, 'Single. Unattached.
Good luck!' Dyan merely gave a smile at the style of
the message rather than its content, she was already
so sure that she could trust him, that he would never
lie to her.

Because they were so seldom alone together, Dyan
hadn't yet told Oliver how she felt, but she was certain
that he knew, just as she was certain that he returned
her love, even though he hadn't yet said so, either.
Both of them were tacitly waiting for the right
moment, the right place, and it wasn't a few minutes
snatched in the shadow of the life-rafts. But when
they were together and Oliver told her how wonderful
she was, how beautiful, how much he wanted her, it

was the headiest of wine, and more than enough to make her completely happy.

Although Dyan wasn't aware of it, and even though she tried to behave towards Oliver in public as a kind of hostess on behalf of Starr Marine, the radiance of being in love gave her away. She sparkled with it like a box of jewels, her green eyes lighting like emeralds when she saw Oliver come into the galley, her cheeks a blush of rubies when he gave her that special look of warm tenderness, her teeth pearls in her constant smile of happiness, and her whole personality diamond bright. The crew, of course, only had to look at her to know what was happening. There were a lot of grins, but they were good-natured ones, because they all liked Dyan, and they tactfully found other things to do when the two of them sat together on the deck, giving them what privacy they could.

The search went methodically on, the only excitement after about ten days when the sonar outlined some irregularities on the sea-bed. Dyan wasn't over-optimistic, they were spread over too wide an area, but thought it was worth a look and sent down a miniature submersible, guided from the ship, and carrying video cameras.

Dyan sat in the ops room, watching the screens as the submersible sank deeper, concentrating all her mind on the task. She was aware that other members of the crew had come into the room and were standing behind her, watching with keen interest, but she didn't look round. Carefully she worked the remote control of the submersible, taking it down almost to the sea-bottom, the sonar map in front of her. The lights from the submersible, flooding the area with brightness, picked out the uneven humps over to the left. She

moved the submersible and something glinted in the
light.

'There!' Oliver's voice came from right behind her
and his hand gripped her shoulder in his eagerness.

Overwhelmed at finding him so close, unnerved by
his touch, Dyan's fingers slipped on the controls and
the submersible spun crazily.

A couple of the men laughed, but Russ said warn-
ingly, 'Watch it, Logan!' and she quickly righted the
robot.

'Sorry. Got carried away,' Oliver apologised.

Dyan murmured an acceptance and turned back to
the screen, trying desperately not to blush, wishing
she had her hair loose so it would hide her face.

The humps turned out to be the wreck of an old
merchant ship, much bigger than the boat they were
looking for. But Dyan noted its position and took
photographs so that she could do some research on
it when they got back to shore, find out if it might
be worth salvaging some time in the future. She
brought the submersible home to the mother-ship and
they resumed their search of the sea-bed as before.

It was a small incident, the way she'd reacted when
Oliver had touched her, but it acted as a catalyst, because that evening after they'd had dinner Oliver stood
up and said in front of the other men who were in
the galley, 'Dyan, come and take a walk on deck with
me,' and he held out his hand to her.

She looked up in surprise, hesitated, not sure how
she was supposed to react.

Oliver made her mind up for her; reaching for her
hand, he pulled her to her feet and put a firm hand
on her waist as he led her out of the cabin. He didn't
speak until they were up on deck, then, as they leaned

against the rail in full view of the bridge, he said, 'Do we have to go on playing this game of pretending that we feel nothing for each other?'

'It isn't a game,' she protested.

'But we're not fooling anyone, you know. Everyone in the ship knows that we're keen on each other.'

'Oh, no, I don't think——'

'Yes, they are,' Oliver insisted. 'Haven't you noticed the way they've started to leave us alone when we're on deck or sitting in the rest room? And I hardly think it's fair on them, when they're being so kind to us, to go on acting as if we're only company representative and client. Do you?'

She gave him a troubled look. 'Has anyone said anything to you? Have they—have they made jokes or remarks?'

'No, of course not. Why should they?'

'I don't want people talking about us,' she said on a suddenly fierce note.

He looked surprised. 'You get on extremely well with the crew. And they don't seem the sort of people to gossip, surely?'

'No, but...' She paused, unable to put her feelings into words. How could she possibly tell him that during her last romance, with Crispin, everyone had known about it, that she had wanted to share her happiness. She had spoken openly of her hopes of being married, but then someone in the company had found out the truth about him while she was at sea, so the information had been sent to Russ, who had tried to break it to her as gently as he could, though he had been full of anger at the man who had deceived her. She had been completely devastated and all the crew had tried to be very kind, very sympathetic. But their kindness had only made things worse, and the rest of that voyage had been hell. So it was little wonder that she wanted to keep her feelings to herself this time.

But that had been before she had got to know Oliver, when she was still wary of being hurt again. But surely, she argued with herself, now that she trusted Oliver it would be possible to acknowledge the fact that she cared about him?

He was waiting in silence, letting her think it through. 'We could perhaps let them know that we quite like each other,' she said tentatively.

'"Quite like each other"! Is that really all you feel?'

'No! You know it isn't.'

'But all you're willing to admit to?'

'To anyone else, yes.'

'And to me?'

Looking up at him, she said softly, 'I don't think I have to tell you. Do I?'

Picking up her hand, he kissed it. 'Yes—because I so very much want to hear you say it. But not now.'

'Because it isn't the right place?' He nodded. 'And that's why this ship isn't the right place for us to—to be more than friends,' she said earnestly.

'Perhaps. But I'm not ashamed of the way I feel about you, Dyan, and I'm not going to act as if I don't care,' he said forcefully. 'Oh, don't worry, I'm not going to try to come to your cabin and make love to you there; I know that would be completely wrong. I'll go on waiting, hard though it is, but as of this moment I want the whole crew to know that I'm interested in, attracted to, and in hot pursuit of you, my lovely one.'

She gave a small, pleased laugh. 'And just how do you intend to do that; shout it from the crow's nest?'

With a smile, Oliver said, 'Oh, no, there's a much simpler way. Like this.' And, taking her in his arms, he gave her a very businesslike kiss.

For a second Dyan was too surprised to move, then she tried to push him away, knowing how easily she succumbed to his embrace, but Oliver's arms tightened about her and he wouldn't let go until she'd been thoroughly kissed, and everyone around had to have seen. That they had was soon evident; as Oliver released her Dyan heard several whistles and cheers.

'Oh! How—how could you?' She stood there, torn between hitting him and bolting for her cabin. But she did neither; seeing the devilment in his eyes, Dyan suddenly saw the funny side of it and began to laugh. 'You have no idea how close you came to having your face slapped,' she told him.

'Oh, yes, I have—but it was definitely worth the risk.'

Strangely, having the crew know somehow relieved the tension between them a little. Now that they didn't have to pretend any more, they were able to spend more time together in open friendliness. Dyan was saved many occasions which had made her blush before: when Oliver had touched her without anyone else seeing, when his eyes had rested on her so caressingly and she had known exactly what he was thinking. The aching need for each other was still there, but there was more opportunity for them to be close, which eased it a little.

Oliver was still just as eager for them to go ashore, and Dyan wanted it too, but there was no reason for them to do so, and she wouldn't take advantage of her position to send the boat in to harbour just to satisfy her own needs. She didn't say this to Oliver, she didn't have to; he was fully aware of her professionalism and didn't even suggest it.

They continued with the search for the next few days, but in the end it was the weather that came to their rescue. A big storm was reported to be brewing up in the area, and although the ship could weather it perfectly well it would make it impossible to continue their steady, parallel-line patrol until it had blown over. The nearest land was the island of St Vincent. With a shaking voice, Dyan gave the order to Russ and he turned the ship and headed for the harbour there.

They reached it around eight in the evening, just as the storm began to break, the wind whipping up the waves. As soon as he knew where they were heading, Oliver had asked to use the phone, so it came as no surprise to Dyan to see a car already waiting on the dock when they arrived.

Going up to the bridge to see Russ, Dyan said, 'It looks as if it won't blow over for at least another twelve hours, so we may as well stay here until about midday tomorrow, and take on fresh food and supplies.' Adding, as the cook hadn't been able to prepare any food in the high seas, 'If any of the crew want to go ashore tonight to eat, that's OK by me. How about you?'

'Yeah. Sure.'

'Tell them the company will pick up the tab.'

'They'll like that.' Russ nodded to the waiting car. 'Is that for you?'

'I think so.'

He gave her a searching look. 'Is it for keeps this time?'

'I hope so. Oh, I *really* hope so.'

'He's a lucky guy, and don't you ever forget that.'

Dyan smiled, and planted a kiss on his rough cheek. 'I'll let you know where I am, in case of emergencies.'

'You think I'm going to let the ship sink when we're tied up in port?' He made a fist at her. 'Get out of my sight, Logan.'

'Aye, aye, Skipper.'

Oliver was waiting for her when she came down below, listening as Russ made the announcement of shore leave over the loudspeaker system. His eyes were full of intense, scarcely suppressed excitement, his face taut, as he said, 'I've booked a room in a hotel ashore. Will you come?'

Her heart gave a great thump and Dyan had to lick lips gone dry before she could nod and say huskily, 'Yes, I'll come with you.'

He put his hand on her shoulder, gripping it tightly, a great flare of triumph in his face. But all he said was, 'See you on the deck in five minutes.'

Hastily she packed a bag, not really knowing what she was putting into it, trying to keep calm and think, but already shaking with anticipation. The storm had driven the sun away and the temperature had dropped considerably, so she pulled on a jacket and then hurried for the companionway.

It had started to rain, large drops that were as yet still warm, but wet you through. But from somewhere Oliver had found a large golf umbrella which he held over her as they ran down the gangplank to the waiting taxi. They dived into it, laughing, dragging the umbrella in after them. Oliver gave a direction to the driver and the car started off. Only then did they really look at each other, the awareness that they were to become lovers at last in their eyes.

'Soon, my darling. Soon,' Oliver murmured, taking her hand in his and carrying it to his lips.

Her fingers tightened on his in excitement. But she said, 'The storm; it's made everything happen so unexpectedly. I thought we would have weeks longer.'

'Does it matter?'

'No, but we would have got to know one another better. There are—there are things I should probably have told you, and——'

Oliver put a finger over her lips, quietening her. 'I know everything I need to know about you. And, anyway, we'll have all the time in the world to learn more about each other. But for now, let's think of nothing but being together at last.'

Perfectly content with that, Dyan opened her mouth and playfully bit his finger.

Immediately Oliver's eyes darkened. 'You minx! I may make you pay for that.' But it was said tenderly, and with a world of promise in his tone.

The hotel was the holiday village type, with individual cabins reached by paths between flowering trees and shrubs, each with a veranda overlooking the shore. But the storm was increasing now and Oliver sighed when they were shown to their cabin and he looked out of the window. 'I wanted this to be perfect for you: moonlight shining on the sand, palm trees... But just look at it! The poor trees are all swaying in the wind, the rain is pelting down, and the sky is so dark that you can hardly see the sea.'

Dyan came to put a hand on his shoulder in a possessive gesture of her own. 'We can close the curtains and shut out the storm, if you want to.' She looked out of the window. 'But I like storms. I like the thunder and lightning, the power and energy of natural phenomena. They're so primitive, so wild.'

'Which is exactly how you make me feel,' Oliver said, his voice thickening as he looked at her. 'I've never wanted a woman the way I want you. So desperately that it's a constant ache in my loins. God, what an old-fashioned word! But there's no other I know to describe the way I feel. It's like a gnawing hunger that won't go away. In the daytime I'm not happy unless you're somewhere in sight; my thoughts are full of you when you're not. And at night—that's the worst of all! I lie in that narrow bed and imagine you just yards away, and I go on thinking about you for most of the night.' He gave a rueful grin. 'I should think the ship is about out of water from all the cold showers I've had to take.'

Dyan smiled in return but her eyes grew tender as she reached up to stroke his face and said, 'You make it sound as if you have some terrible fever.'

'I have.' He caught her hand and kissed the palm. 'And there's only one known cure.'

'And when you're cured?' Her eyes were questioning.

Immediately understanding, he said, 'But I don't think I ever will be. You've lit a fire in me, my beautiful one, that will never go out.'

A group of people, clad only in swimsuits, ran past in front of the window, frolicking in the rain, making them draw apart, laughing.

'The only way to dress in this weather,' Oliver said with a grin as he drew the curtains.

There was a trolley with champagne in a bucket of ice and several covered dishes, standing over by a table. Going to it, Dyan lifted one of the lids. There was a big serving plate of hors d'oeuvres: small shellfish, cornets of ham and caviar, anchovies, and salmon flown from Scotland.

'I thought we might get hungry,' Oliver explained, coming to open the champagne. He poured some into the two glasses and handed one to her.

Dyan watched the bubbles settle, feeling, even though she was eager and happy, suddenly shy. Like a bride on her wedding-night, she thought, with self-mockery. But that *was* how she felt, because all the past was as nothing now; whatever had gone before: Crispin, the mistakes she'd made, didn't matter one iota. All that mattered was the here and now, as they stood together, alone at last. That there was a raging storm instead of tropical moonlight was incidental, even that they only had one night before they must return to the ship; all that was forgotten as they raised their glasses in a toast that had no need for words because their eyes, dark with shared need, said it all.

They drank, but then Oliver reached out and took the glass from her unsteady hand, putting them down clumsily so that they spilt. His eyes, hot with yearning, devoured her. He undid her hair, letting it fall heavy on her shoulders. 'Dyan.' He said her name on a hoarse, ragged note, and put his hands on either side of her face. 'I love you. I'm crazy about you! And, oh, God, I want you so much!'

A great swell of happiness filled her heart, and Dyan tried to tell him that she felt the same, but suddenly Oliver could wait no longer and dragged her to him, kissing her fiercely, bending her body against his as his mouth took hers in savage insistence.

His hands were on her clothes, pulling off her jacket. He tried to be gentle, but wanted her so badly that his shaking hands tore at the buttons of her blouse and fumbled with the catch of her bra. But then his hands were on her skin, cupping her breasts, and she moaned as she arched towards him, her mass of red hair cascading down her back. He bent to kiss her, making her cry out, and then his hands went to the rest of her clothes, kissing her as he took them off. When she stood naked before him, he looked up at her, wonder in his eyes.

'You're so beautiful, my darling. So lovely.'

Slowly he rose, his hands trailing up her body, sending great waves of desire coursing through her, making her give small, animal-like sounds of tormented frustration. He kissed her mouth, and she could feel his body trembling, his breath rasping in his throat. Somehow his clothes joined hers on the floor, although she wasn't sure who, between their eager hands, had taken off what. Oliver's body was deeply tanned now, even the part where his swimming trunks had covered. He stood tall and bronzed and godlike in the light of the lamps. His body eager to take her. The most overwhelming picture of arrogant masculinity.

Her eyes were full of awe, and she must have made some sound. Oliver glanced down at himself, then, his jaw rigid as he strove for control, he pulled her to him and kissed her with deep, deep tenderness. 'I won't hurt you. I love you,' he said between kisses. Then he held her a little away from him. 'And you?'

She smiled because she knew that he already knew the answer, loved him even more because he could stop and ask at such a moment. 'Of course I love you, you idiot,' she assured him. And added urgently, 'And now, for God's sake...'

He gave a rich burst of laughter and happiness, caught her by the waist and lifted her above him. But then his eyes filled with a great fire and he carried her to the bed and dropped her on to it. For a brief moment he stood over her, looking down at her female loveliness, but then he gave a groan and came down on to her, taking her with all the wild abandon of a primitive savage, as tempestuously as the storm.

That first time they were too out of control to care much about the other, both greedy for this end to the aching frustration, wanting only to be a part of each other, to satiate themselves in sexual fulfilment. They both found excitement, but it was over too quickly, and it was the next time, when the need wasn't as urgent, when they could explore each other's bodies with caressing hands and lips, that they shared a great, explosive climax of physical love.

Afterwards, their bodies hot and damp, Dyan lay in his arms, knowing that this was the happiest, most contented moment of her life. She'd thought that Crispin was a good lover, but compared to what she had just experienced. . .! Dyan pushed that thought out of her mind, not wanting to think about her old flame. And anyway, how could it possibly have been so good when this was love and that had only been a sham?

With his free arm, Oliver pushed the hair from her damp forehead, kissed her eyes, her nose. 'Would you like a drink?'

She nodded and he got up to refill their glasses.

'To you, my wonderful darling,' he said as he got back beside her. 'I just knew you'd be a wildcat in bed.'

'We're not exactly in it,' she pointed out with a smile.

'Do you want to get under the covers?'

'No. I'm too hot.'

'So I noticed.' Lifting a finger, Oliver traced it down her throat and to the tip of her breast, making the nipple rise. He smiled and bent to kiss it. 'From the moment I met you I knew you were all fire and sensuality under that cool act you put on.'

'How could you know?'

'Don't you recall what I told you: that I'd always remember the moment I fell for you? It was because you looked so amazing when you were angry, like a tigress.'

'Did I really get angry?'

He nodded and took a drink. 'Standing up for your rights and determined to be treated with equality; the suffragettes would have been proud of you.'

'Well, you threw me,' Dyan said by way of excuse. 'I was expecting an old, pompous martinet—and instead I got you.' She gave him a wicked glance. 'A young, pompous, martin—oh!' She gasped as he poured a little wine on her breast and bent to lick it off. 'Hey, watch it, buster. Do that again and you might find yourself being attacked.'

'If you will issue a challenge,' Oliver murmured, and did it again.

Putting down her glass, retaliation in her eyes, Dyan took his glass from him and put it aside, then pushed him back against the pillows. 'You asked for this.' She let her hand stroke across his chest, teasing him as she toyed with his own tiny nipples, knowing it was too soon and she was safe. Her hand moved on, outlining the slim athletic waist and the flat plane of his stomach. It stopped as she realised, and she said, 'How come you're brown all over? You always wear your shorts on the ship.'

He laughed. 'Haven't you found out yet? Most of the crew sunbathe in the nude when you're not around. They have someone stationed at the companionway who gives a warning whistle whenever you're coming on deck. Then there's a mad scramble to get their shorts on.' He looked at her and his grin broadened. 'You did know?'

'Of course. I've always known. A couple of times I came up on deck too quickly and I've had to "remember" something and go back down for a few minutes.' She gave him a saucy look and ran her hand over him. 'But you measure up pretty well, Balfour.'

'Do I, indeed?'

His eyes darkened dangerously, and when he pulled her on top of him, she found that it wasn't safe after all.

This time it was all for her. Oliver touched her, kissed her, as if she were an instrument on which he was playing the most exquisite tune. Forgetting his own need, he used his body for her pleasure, bringing her close to a climax but then away again, not once, but several times, until she moaned and panted, head thrown back in ecstasy, her fingers digging into his back as she writhed under him. Just as she thought that she couldn't stand it any longer, that she would go mad with this ravishment of her senses, he thrust hard and brought her to such a pitch of pleasure that she cried out like a wild thing, her breath a long, shuddering groan of sensuous wonder, giving her delight such as she had never known. Only then, did he

relax his iron control and let his body take its own
fulfilment.

Afterwards she lay limp in his arms, tears of
gratitude on her cheeks, while he lay breathless and
panting beside her.

'Oh, Oliver,' she said on a note of continued
wonder. 'I didn't know. I had no idea.'

Turning on his side, he kissed her and said raggedly,
'Have you ever been in love before? Have you?'

He had said that he didn't want to know about her
past, but she recognised in his voice the intense need
of a lover to be sure that he was the only one who
mattered, now or in the past. A fleeting thought of
her last romance came into Dyan's mind, but that
hadn't been love even though she'd thought so at the
time. It had been nothing compared to this. So she
said with utter assurance and certainty, 'Oh, no. Only
you. Only you, my darling, my love.'

Oliver smiled, kissed her, and almost immediately
fell asleep. Dyan looked down at him for quite a while,
thinking how radically life could change in such a
relatively short time. A couple of months ago she had
been a career-girl with a strong determination to stay
that way; now, if Oliver asked her, she would will-
ingly give up everything to be with him. She had a
fleeting feeling of guilt that she was letting the side
down, but no woman with a lover like Oliver was
going to stay on in a job that would keep her from
his side for months at a time. Dyan gave a cat-like
grin. Having sampled the goods, she was definitely
hooked!

And she was definitely hungry. Getting off the bed
she carefully put her side of the coverlet over Oliver,
in case he got cold, then went into the bathroom where

she showered and put on the hotel bath-robe she found there. The food was delicious. Greedily, Dyan piled a plate and poured herself a fresh glass of champagne, then went to sit on the bed again, her back against the soft headboard. Dreamily, she ate and drank, gazing into space, seeing there a future of complete happiness.

Oliver stirred and blinked against the light. Opening his eyes, he smiled at the sight of her. 'I suppose I'll be lucky if you've left me a few crumbs,' he said in mock complaint, sitting up.

'I was so hungry—starving.'

'That's what good sex does for you.'

'*Great* sex,' she corrected him.

He sat up and was helping himself from her plate, but quickly looked at her. 'Was it?'

'You know it was.' She gave a small laugh. 'I think you must have practised quite a bit to get that good.'

'Do you mind?'

Her eyes widened. '*Are you crazy*?'

Oliver laughed and took a stuffed date from her plate.

'Hey!' She moved the plate away. 'Get your own.'

'Tyrant! Why have you got that thing on?' he complained. 'Take it off.' She obliged and he kissed her shoulder. 'You smell clean and gorgeous.'

'I had a shower while you were asleep.'

'Don't you feel tired?'

'No, I've never been more awake in my life,' she said with sincerity.

Lifting his hand he began to toy with her hair, winding it around his fingers. 'I'm crazy about your hair. I think it was the first thing about you that I fell in love with. Or perhaps your eyes, spitting fire at me.' He gave a reminiscent smile. 'When I first met you and you told me your name, I thought that you were married and I had to control my disappointment. I couldn't believe that anyone as gorgeous as you was still free. Any man in his right senses would have snapped you up long ago.'

'I'm choosy,' she told him.

'Well, I hope I come up to your expectations.'

'Keep trying; I'll let you know.'

He gave a roar of laughter. 'God, I love you!' He kissed her shoulder again. 'Are you going to sit there and eat all night?'

Her eyebrows rose. 'I thought you were hungry?'

'I am,' he said, holding her eyes.

'Oh.' She smiled and put the plate aside, but said chidingly, 'Man cannot live on love alone, you know.'

'This one can,' Oliver said firmly, pulling her down beside him.

The storm had passed and brilliant sunshine sent rays of light across the room in the chinks between the curtains when Dyan woke the next morning. Oliver was still asleep, but held her possessively in his arms. It wasn't the first time she had woken that morning, but the last time she had been facing Oliver, and when she'd moved, he had woken and pulled her to him, making love to her as she lay in the bed beside him. So now she carefully lifted her arm to look at her watch, and found that it was nearly eleven o'clock.

'Oliver! Hey, wake up.' She shook him awake.

'What is it?' Putting his hand behind her head he pulled her down to kiss her.

She returned it for a moment, but said, 'We have no time for that.'

'You're joking.' And he kissed her again.

Laughing against his mouth, she said, 'I mean it. We're late. We have to get back to the ship.'

Sitting up, he looked at his own watch, then stiffened. 'What day is it?'

'Tuesday,' Dyan told him, laughing. 'You haven't been to sleep that long!'

'No, I mean what's the date?'

'The twenty-fourth.'

'Good grief! What time is it in England?'

'About seven o'clock in the morning, I think. Oh, no, they put the clocks forward for summer, so it could be eight.'

'Then I've just time.'

'For what?'

'It's my mother's birthday, and we have this sort of tradition that I always call her first thing. And I must arrange for some flowers to be sent, too. I can probably do that from reception better than here. Do you mind if I shower first?'

'No, of course not. Go ahead. What about breakfast?'

'I'll wait for lunch.'

He was soon out of the shower, and dressed while Dyan had hers. Putting his head round the shower curtain, he said, 'I'll be back as soon as I can.' Then gave a groan as he looked at her soap-lathered body. 'Lord, I wish I could rub that over you. Heaven knows when we're going to be able to be together like this again.' Unable to resist, he leaned in and got wet as he kissed her breast, then groaned as he tore himself away.

Buoyantly, radiantly happy, Dyan dressed and ate some more of the food as she did so. Oliver seemed to be taking a long time. Uneasily she glanced at her watch, not wanting to be late back at the ship, knowing that it was going to be embarrassing going back there together as it was. He had been gone nearly half an hour before the phone rang and she rushed to answer it. 'Yes? Hello,' she said eagerly.

'Miss Logan, this is Reception. We have a message for you from Mr Balfour. He's been delayed and he asked that you go back to the ship ahead of him. There's a cab here waiting for you.'

'Is Mr Balfour there? Can I speak to him?'

'I'm sorry, he's using another phone.'

'I see. OK, I'll be right over.'

Picking up their bags, she walked quickly over to the main building. Inside she left Oliver's bag with the receptionist. Looking round, she saw him sitting in one of the booths, but he had his back to her and looked to be talking earnestly. She would have gone over but she didn't want to disturb him and it was too late to wait, so she went out to the taxi and was driven back to the ship.

Luckily a lorry full of supplies had just arrived as she got to the dock, and the watch were busy unloading it, so she was able to hurry up the gangplank. It was easier for her going back alone; there were a few raised eyebrows but no knowing smiles. She dumped her things in her cabin, plaited her hair, and went to the galley for some orange juice. From there she could see out onto the dock, so sat and watched for Oliver to arrive.

He was late getting back; they were loaded and ready to go. Dyan began to experience an entirely new emotion, that of fear that something might have happened to him, an accident or something, and she gave a sigh of relief when another taxi drove up to the quay and Oliver got out. Quickly she ran up on deck, eager just to see and speak to him again. He strode up the gangplank, gave a quick nod of apology to the first mate who was standing at its head, and walked towards the companionway where Dyan was standing. She smiled at him, her eyes full of the love that they'd shared.

Oliver glanced at her—and gave her a look that showed revulsion in every hard line of his face, a look of utter disgust and loathing, a look that shrivelled her soul. Then he strode on past her without a word.

CHAPTER FIVE

'Is IT OK to leave, boss?' The crewman frowned and raised his voice. 'Dyan? Is it OK to set sail now?'

She stared at him unseeingly, her eyes round and numb with shock.

Putting his hand on her arm, he gave her a small shake. 'Dyan, are you OK? The skipper wants to know if we can sail now?'

She blinked, the words at last penetrating, and managed to nod. The crewman gave her an uneasy look, but went hurrying back to give the go-ahead to Russ. The engine started, the mooring lines were released and the ship eased slowly and gently out from the quay, across the harbour and into the open sea, giving two blasts of the horn as they passed the entrance. The grey storm clouds had completely disappeared and the sky was its usual clear, deep blue, and the sea at its calmest with only the occasional leaping barracuda breaking the surface.

Going over to the rail, Dyan leaned against it, her back to the ship, trying to get her brain working, trying desperately to work things out. Not for an instant did she pretend to herself that she had been mistaken, that Oliver had been thinking of something else and had just happened to glance her way. No, he'd meant it all right. She clutched the rail as she remembered. Never, in all her life, had anyone given her a look of such intense loathing. She'd never given anyone cause to do so. And for the life of her she couldn't think what she'd done to make Oliver look at her like that now. Especially after last night. It had been so good, so wonderful. Dyan bit hard on her bottom lip, feeling completely devastated by what had happened. To have been so radiantly happy, so sure of Oliver and of her future, and to have it all shattered within the space of an hour...

Something must have happened to make him change so completely; it was the only reason Dyan could think of. But what it was she had absolutely no idea. Everything had been fine until he'd gone off to phone his mother. Could his mother have been taken ill or even died and they'd been trying to contact him? If they'd been unable to reach him, in his grief, Oliver might possibly have blamed her for putting him out of contact. But no, that couldn't be, because she'd phoned the ship and left the number of the hotel in case of any emergency. And, although she hadn't said so, everyone in the crew must have had a darn good idea that Oliver was with her. If an urgent message had come for him they surely would have rung? But it was still a remote possibility, so Dyan went straight down to the ops room, almost running in her hurry, and turned on the machine that recorded all incoming calls.

There was nothing. No calls for Oliver or anyone else.

So what the hell had happened then? Dyan gazed down at the desk, going back over the night, torturing her mind to remember if it was something that she'd done. But always it came back to the same thing; everything had been great until Oliver had left her to phone home. So it had to be something he'd heard during his phone call, or in the hotel lobby in the half-hour that he'd been away from her. Then she remembered that he'd made more than one call. Perhaps he'd taken the opportunity to ring his office in London. Maybe it had been something he'd been told then that had made him so angry. A power struggle? A rival taking advantage of his absence to usurp his position, or something? That would, of course, make him angry, but how could he possibly blame her for it? And if that was so, why had he come back to the ship? Surely his immediate reaction would have been to get on the first available plane back to England so he could fight it out?

Nothing added up. With a sinking heart Dyan realised that there was only going to be one way she could find out; by asking Oliver straight out what was the matter. Well, she had the right to do that. By taking her to bed, Oliver had created a degree of intimacy in their relationship that gave her a moral claim on him. Or an immoral claim, she thought with sudden, twisted humour, a self-inflicted hurt. But how to ask him, and when? For a moment her heart shrank from the task, because she knew that another look of loathing from him would destroy her. But Dyan wasn't a coward and she knew that to go and confront him right now was the only way. Besides, anything was better than not knowing, anything better than this self-torture of conjecture.

She stood up to go, but the door opened and Russ came in, firmly closing the door behind him and leaning his broad back against it.

'You OK, Logan?'

Putting her hands behind her she gripped the edge of the desk, and from somewhere managed the travesty of a smile. 'Sure. Fine. Why do you ask?'

'You haven't been up to the bridge to give us our heading.'

'Oh.' She frowned, trying to drag her mind back to her job. 'Sorry. I—er—I just took it that you'd head back for where we left off before the storm.'

'Yeah, I did that.'

'So what's the problem?' she said on an impatient note, eager, now that she'd taken the decision, to go and confront Oliver.

'I haven't got a problem—but I thought maybe you had.'

'What gives you that idea?' she said with difficulty.

'Andy said you looked like a zombie, that you were as white as a ghost.'

Her nails digging into the hard surface of the desk, Dyan tried to keep her voice light as she said, 'He must have the supernatural on the brain. Comes of watching too many horror films.'

Russ gave her a searching look. 'You went off with Balfour last night.'

'So?'

'So—did something happen between you two?'

She knew that he was being kind, that he cared about her, but there was no way Dyan could talk to anyone about this, not now, probably not ever, so she deliberately let her face and voice harden as she said, 'That's none of your business, Russ. And now, if you don't mind, I have some work to do,' she added, pointedly moving towards the door.

For a moment Russ hesitated, searching her face, and Dyan's heart sank because she knew he was quite capable of just folding his arms and refusing to move until she'd told him the truth. But, thankfully, he decided not to pursue it and moved aside to let her precede him out of the office. Outside, in the ops room, she pulled out a chart at random and spread it on the table, bending over to study it as if her life depended on knowing every inch of it. Russ watched her for a moment, then walked to the door, but turned as he reached it and said, 'Alaska was the last trip, Logan!' then walked out the door.

For a moment she didn't understand, then looked down at the chart properly and saw that she'd been studying the cold Arctic Ocean rather than the hot Caribbean Sea. So she hadn't fooled Russ for a minute. Dyan sighed and rolled up the chart, put it away. It took a few minutes to work up the courage again, but then, bracing her shoulders, she made for Oliver's cabin.

She knocked but there was no answer. Thinking he might not have heard, she knocked again, harder this time, rapping her knuckles against the door. Still no answer. It came to her that he might have guessed it was her, that he might be deliberately ignoring her. On a wave of anger she threw the door open and strode in. The cabin was empty, the bed still made from yesterday, all Oliver's belongings stowed neatly away. It was the first time she'd been in his cabin, one of the larger ones on the ship, and despite her present turmoil of emotions she was able to take in the absence of any personal belongings lying around. There were no photographs, and only a couple of books on the shelf above his bed, borrowed from the ship's small library. The only thing of his was the documents case that stood on its side beside the small work-table. It all seemed so impersonal, as if Oliver hadn't wanted to stamp his personality on the room.

Dyan stood indecisively, wondering whether to wait or to go in search of him. Angrily she realised that there were so few places on the ship where it was possible to have a private conversation. It had to be in a cabin or in the office in the ops room. There was nowhere else. It wasn't even possible to talk on the deck without being overheard unless you walked down to where the submersible was stored. So what should she do?

The decision was taken out of her hands as the galley bell sounded throughout the ship, letting the crew know that lunch was ready. Quickly she came out of Oliver's cabin and closed the door, strode to her own cabin. Once inside she turned and beat her fists against the bulkhead in an agony of uncertainty. Would Oliver go to the galley? Would she have to face him for the first time with all the crew who weren't on watch looking on? All her life Dyan had known what she wanted and had gone for it. Back on the island, in the hotel room, she had also been sure of what she wanted, but now all her certainty and self-confidence seemed to have drained from her and she found it impossible to make up her mind.

In the end it was habit that won; they would all expect her to eat with them so that was what she would do. When the world turned upside down, clinging to the daily ritual could be a life-saver.

In a heightened state of awareness, Dyan thought she noticed a few of the men look at her more closely than usual as she walked in. Her immediate response was to smile as if she hadn't a care in the world and take her place at the table. A second's glance had told her that Oliver wasn't there. Maybe he wouldn't come. Maybe he—— There was the sound of voices and

Oliver came in with two of the crew, all of them talking as if they were finishing a conversation. It wasn't a fixed habit, but during the last week or so Oliver had always sat next to her, eager for her company. A place had been left for him now and she looked to see if he would join her. He finished his conversation, glanced round the room. His eyes, cold and impersonal, passed over her, and he deliberately went to sit in a vacant place at the other end of the big table.

Someone else sat next to her. A plate was put in front of Dyan and she automatically picked up a fork and began to eat, but the food tasted like sawdust in her mouth and she couldn't swallow it. Looking down the table, she saw that Oliver was talking in apparent ease to the man next to him. Dyan wanted to scream out, What is it? What have I done? but she had to just sit there and try to pretend that nothing had happened.

Russ was at the table and she realised that he was watching her. Flashing him an overbright smile, she managed to eat a couple more mouthfuls, then pushed the plate away. She glanced again at Oliver but he had his head turned away, deliberately avoiding her eyes.

The meal was the longest Dyan had ever known, but somehow she sat through it. Not until everyone was finished and moving away from the table did she leave the galley and go to the ops room. As always there was a man on duty at the radar screen. Snapping the words out as an order, Dyan said to him, 'Go and tell Mr Balfour I want to see him here immediately. Don't take no for an answer. Then stay out until I send for you.'

The crewman looked at her in astonishment, used to receiving his orders in a more civilised tone and with a 'please' tagged on the end. But he rose at once and went to obey her.

It was almost ten minutes before Oliver came to the cabin, standing in the doorway as he said, 'You wanted to see me?'

'Close the door.'

Slowly he did so, but he didn't come into the room, just stood on the threshold, his hands thrust in his pockets, his shoulder leaning against the wall. 'Well?'

Dyan looked at him closely, her eyes searching his face for any signs of the love that he'd professed in the night, but his features were hard, implacable, and his eyes still held the contempt she'd seen earlier. Her heart filled with despair but her chin came up as she said, 'I want to know just what the hell is going on?'

'Going on?' He deliberately chose to misunderstand her. 'Nothing, as far as I'm concerned.'

Striving to keep all pathos, all pleading out of her voice, she said, 'Don't treat me like some brainless moron; why have you changed towards me?'

'I beg your pardon,' Oliver said in a deep sarcasm. 'Was that what I was doing? It wasn't my intention, I assure you. If anything, I prefer not to have anything to do with you at all.'

Even though she'd almost been expecting something like this it still came as a shock to hear him say it. Dyan stared at him, fighting hard not to let him see how hurt she was. But her voice was unsteady as she jerked out, 'That wasn't what you said last night.'

Oliver's face grew glacially cold. 'Last night was a mistake,' he said curtly.

Dyan had never known such emotional pain in all her life, but with the pain came anger and she said shortly, 'So it would appear—especially on my part.' His trousers were tight across his hips and she saw his hands, inside his pockets, clench into fists. So he hadn't liked that. Good!

But he said sharply, 'So let's say that we both made a mistake. That should leave you free to run around after every other man that comes your way, shouldn't it?'

Colour rose in her cheeks. 'I don't deserve that from you.'

Again the look of intense loathing came into his face, tearing at her heart. 'You deserve every insult you get.' He paused, then added with deliberate contempt, 'You cheap little tramp. You *slut*!'

He waited for her to answer him, to retaliate, but Dyan just stood there staring at him, as if turned to stone, unable to believe he'd called her such cruel, foul names. Oliver gave a cynical smile, turned, and walked out of the room.

When she finally stirred, Dyan moved more like a clockwork doll than a human being, walking stiffly, as if she didn't know how to use her limbs. Going to the door, she called the crewman in, and left him there as she went to her own cabin. Two of the divers were standing in the corridor as she went by, and moved out of her way. They looked at her in surprise and one of them spoke to her, but she didn't hear. Her ears were still full of the insults that Oliver had thrown at her, her brain benumbed by them. When she reached her cabin she just sat down on the bed, her back rigid, her hands balled so tightly her nails dug deeply into her skin, but that was a far lesser pain than the one in her heart and she didn't even feel it.

They reached the area where they'd been searching before the storm and the ship resumed its former search pattern. Usually Dyan would have been either up on deck or in the ops room, but that afternoon she stayed in her cabin, too hurt to face anyone. She would have liked to stay there all evening, too, but around five Russ came down and hammered on her door.

'Dyan? Come on, open up.'

Knowing that she couldn't tell him to go away, that he wouldn't go even if she did, Dyan pushed herself to her feet and opened the door.

Russ came in carrying a bottle and a couple of glasses. He kicked the door shut behind him and put the glasses on her chest of drawers as he opened the bottle and poured out a hefty measure. 'Here. Drink this.'

'What is it?'

He showed her the label. 'Bottle of my best cognac.'

He lowered his big frame into the only chair and Dyan sat down on the bed again. 'You only drink that on special occasions.'

'It got back to me that you looked as if you could do with a drink—and only the best is good enough for you, Logan,' he added deliberately.

She thanked him with her eyes and took a long swallow. It felt like fire in her mouth but the after-taste was nectar. 'I could get used to this,' she murmured.

'Drink up. There's plenty more.'

Leaning back against the bulkhead she said, 'You trying to get me drunk, Skipper?'

'Do you want to get drunk?'

'I think this is the closest I ever came to wanting to.' But then she shook her head. 'No, it wouldn't solve anything.'

'What is there to solve?'

She smiled a little, a bitter twist of her lips. 'I haven't the faintest idea. No, I'm not trying to tell you to mind your own business this time,' she said quickly as she saw him frown. 'I just honestly don't know what I'm supposed to have done to—to...'

'To Balfour?'

'To turn him against me.' She leaned forward and gave Russ a pleading look. 'What is it, Russ? What is it about me that always attracts the wrong men? Yesterday he was crazy for me, but now—now he looks at me as if he hates and despises me. But I don't know what I've done!' She turned away, biting her lip, for the first time close to tears.

'Why don't you just come right out and ask him?'

'I did.' Her face blanched as she remembered.

'And?'

The knuckles holding the glass showed white. 'I— it doesn't matter.'

Russ gave her a shrewd look. 'Listen, don't get mad at me; but did you sleep with him?'

She hesitated, but the hesitation gave her away. With an angry shrug she said, 'Yes, of course I did. Why the hell shouldn't I? I'm twenty-six years old and I— I was in love with him. Why, you even said yourself that you liked him! And I thought—he said...' She bit her lip again, the hurt and misery patent in her eyes.

'He told you he was in love with you?' Dyan nodded dumbly and Russ swore aloud. 'The bastard! Wait till I get my hands on him, I'll——'

'No!' Dyan grabbed his arm as he started to get to his feet, vengeance in his angry eyes. 'No, I won't let you.' She pulled him back into his chair. 'Promise me that you won't hurt him. *Please*, Russ. You've got to let me have some dignity, some pride. Can't you see that's all I have left?'

She was gripping his arm so tightly that he could feel it through his denim shirt. He nodded. 'Yeah, you're right. It wouldn't do.' He hesitated, then said, 'Logan, I've got to say this to you. You may be all of twenty-six, but you're a real greenhorn when it comes to men. How many men have you had in your life? I bet it's just the two; that other English guy and now Balfour. Am I right?'

Her face white, Dyan gave a brief nod.

'I thought so.' Russ sighed. 'Look, there are some guys who're only interested in a girl until they get her. They enjoy the chase, and they'll do anything to get a woman, tell her anything they think she wants to hear. And mostly a woman wants to hear a man say that he's in love with her. Because that's a woman's power. The only one she has over a man. Or sometimes a guy will tell the girl he loves her while they're having sex, because at that moment he probably does love her because she's making him happy. Do you understand what I'm saying?' She nodded again and he went on, 'But the last thing that guy wants is to hear the girl telling him *she loves him*. Because then he can see himself getting hooked. Home, mortgage, kids, medical bills—that's mostly what marriage means to a guy. And that's a big price to pay for a night's sex.'

Russ had put it crudely, perhaps deliberately, cutting her big romance down to the small and sordid thing it probably was. With great difficulty she said, 'And you think that Oliver was like that? That—that he just wanted me sexually, because I was there and—and available?'

'It sure sounds like it to me.'

With bitter self-flagellation she said, 'Well, he certainly had reason to call me a cheap tramp, then. Because I didn't fight him off at all. I thought—I really thought...' She broke off and put a hand up to her face as the tears spilled over at last.

'Here, drink some more.' Russ filled her glass up again. His face grim, he said, 'Did he really call you that?'

'*And some,*' she said bitterly. But after she'd taken a drink Dyan managed to stop crying and shook her head in vexation. 'I didn't mean to tell you that. Promise me that you won't tell anyone.' He didn't say yes at once so she said forcefully, 'I mean it, Russ. I have to cope with this on my own.'

He nodded reluctantly. 'Yeah, OK. But look, he probably didn't mean it. He just wanted to scare you off. Turn you against him, in case you got any ideas about a permanent relationship.'

'He isn't married,' Dyan put in. 'I checked. I at least had enough sense to do that, after the last time.'

Russ shrugged. 'So he isn't married. That doesn't mean he hasn't got his eye on some girl in England. Or maybe he just wants to marry someone who could be useful to him in his career. Limeys still go for that kind of thing, don't they?'

'Not any that I'd want to know,' she said with feeling. She gave him an uncertain look. 'Am I such a bad judge of character, Russ? First Crispin and now—now this.'

'Hell, no.' He put out his large rough hand and patted hers comfortingly. 'When you meet a guy and fall for him, you're just too honest to hide what you feel. And they've taken advantage of that. They're the creeps, not you.' He gave her an encouraging grin. 'Maybe third time lucky, huh?'

'Oh, no,' Dyan said bitterly. 'This time I really have learnt my lesson. I'm *never* going to let another man into my life.'

'Now look, Logan, you don't want to talk like that. You never know——' He broke off as the telephone rang.

Dyan picked it up, listened, said, 'OK, I'll be right there.' Putting the phone down she turned to Russ. 'They've got an interesting trace on the sonar scan.'

She splashed water on her face and looked at herself in the mirror as she dried it, thanking God that there were no tell-tale tear stains.

'You look OK,' Russ told her, but held out her glass. 'Finish this.'

She obeyed him and managed a wobbly smile. 'Thanks for coming to my rescue,' she said huskily, but caught his arm as he turned away. 'Remember what you promised: that you won't hurt him or say anything.'

'Sure, I remember.' He opened the door for her but as she went out ahead of him, he said under his breath, 'But there's more than one way to skin a cat.'

The trace looked hopeful, much more interesting than the previous one they'd found. The area it covered was smaller and the vessel looked almost intact.

Dyan glanced at her watch. 'We should just have time to send the video cameras down before it gets dark.'

From behind her, Oliver said, 'Surely it's completely dark at the bottom of the sea at all times of the day? So what difference does it make whether you send the cameras down in daytime or at night?'

Her face tightening, Dyan said to the first mate, 'Tell Russ we're sending down the robot, then lower it overboard.' Only then did she turn to Oliver and say in a coldly patient tone, 'You're quite right, it is always dark on the bottom, but it's much safer for the crew to work in daylight. If we worked at night we'd have to have the floodlights on, and you may have noticed that we're still quite close to the shipping lanes; another ship, seeing us, might well come over to take a look at what we're doing. If it is the *Xanadu*, don't you think it would be better not to give away its position?'

'I see. Thank you for putting it so succinctly.' There was sarcasm in his tone, veiled, but not enough, so that the members of the crew who were in the room looked first at him and then at Dyan, their eyebrows raised.

Although it wasn't necessary, Dyan went up on deck to watch the robot being lowered, angrily aware that by now most of the crew would know that she and Oliver had quarrelled. But there was nothing she could do about that, because for the life of her she couldn't behave towards him as if nothing had happened, the hurt was too great. All she could hope was that he would keep out of her way so that she didn't have the agony of seeing him too often.

But he was still in the ops room when she went back, and stood behind her with some of the other men while they watched the film sent back by the robot. It looked good, really promising. The sunken vessel was about the the right size and looked fairly new, but they couldn't see the name because the recent storm, and those throughout the winter, had stirred the sand and already partly covered it. Despite her personal troubles, Dyan felt the familiar *frisson* of excitement that she always got when they found what they were looking for. And if it was the *Xanadu*, then her figures had been correct: it was within a couple of miles of the centre of the area she'd worked out.

Russ's hand tightened on her shoulder. 'Well done, Logan. Looks as if you've found our drowned duck.'

'It looks promising,' she admitted. 'We'll get the robot up and send the submersible down early tomorrow morning for a closer look.'

'Good.' Russ gave the necessary orders to the Mate over the phone. 'Now let's have some chow.'

In the galley, Dyan unexpectedly found herself very popular. A drink was put in her hand as they waited for the cook to sound the bell, and Hal and another two men stood round her, almost like a human wall, completely monopolising her. But Dyan was tall enough to look over their shoulders and see Oliver come into the cabin. He went to join the group nearest him, but the men turned their backs, deliberately shutting him out, as did the next man he turned to speak to.

With a surge of dismay, Dyan realised what was happening; the men had all become partisan on her behalf, had decided to shut Oliver out to show their disapproval. Well, Dyan certainly had no reason to show him any politeness, but it was *her* that he'd used so badly, and *she* was the only one who had the right to snub him, not the men, however well-intentioned. She made a move to step out of the circle of men around her, but it was too late; Oliver saw her looking at him and gave her a small, infinitely sardonic bow, according her a victory that she hadn't instigated and would have been ashamed to win.

It was the same at dinner. Dyan was seated, willy-nilly, between Russ and Hal, their large frames acting almost as a shield, while Oliver was pointedly avoided. When he sat down at the end of the table, the man next to him got up and moved to another place. Oliver made no comment, and showed very little reaction beyond another sardonic glance in Dyan's direction. He left the galley immediately after dinner, to go back to his cabin, Dyan presumed. She was challenged to a game of poker with some of the men, which she accepted, recognising that they were trying to help her. But she couldn't concentrate, and after about an hour excused herself and went up on deck.

The moon was its usual shining silver disc. Glancing up at it, Dyan wished that the night had been dark and overcast, then it wouldn't have reminded her so much of the times she and Oliver had met up here to steal a half-hour or so together. It had all seemed so romantic, so wonderful. But now... Vainly trying to put the hurt and bitterness out of her mind, Dyan found that it was impossible to think rationally. Her values, her confidence in herself were all shot to pieces. She had been so sure of Oliver, but now she doubted if she would ever be able to trust a man again, not

where emotions came into it. It would have been very
easy, when she was feeling so low, to blame herself,
to think that it was something that she'd done, or just
something within her, that had made him turn against
her. But some inner voice made her realise that she
mustn't do that, or she would crack up completely.
I've got to fight this, she told herself. But it was so
difficult when she didn't really know why Oliver had
turned against her so suddenly and completely. Russ
had said it was probably because he was that type of
man, but she still couldn't believe that she had been
so completely mistaken in him.

Irritably, knowing that she was getting nowhere and
that such thoughts would drive her mad, Dyan turned
and walked down the length of the deck to where the
big submersible was stored, seeing her way clearly in
the moonlight. She looked it over, making sure the
davits that would lower it over the side were well-
greased, not wanting any hitches tomorrow. Yesterday
she had wanted the voyage to go on forever, now all
she wanted was to find the *Xanadu* and to get back
to port as quickly as possible.

The seaman on watch came up and they exchanged
a quiet greeting before he continued on his round towards the other end of the ship. Dyan gave the submersible a last check and walked back up the port
side towards the nearest companionway. The dark
shadow of one of the lifeboats was like a black pool
through which she had to pass. As she did so a voice
came out of the darkness, harsh and scathing,
'Looking for me?'

She jumped, not having been able to see Oliver as
he leaned against the rail. For a moment she was
overcome by surprise, but his arrogant assumption

that she might still want to seek him out after the way he'd treated her, made her angry enough to retort contemptuously, '*You*? You must be joking.'

It was impossible to see his face in this shadowed place, but he didn't sound put out, just heavily sarcastic as he said, 'Really? Then just which poor fool did you come up here to meet?'

Aware of the seaman on duty, Dyan kept her voice low, but it was vibrant with anger as she said, 'You have no reason and no right to speak to me like that.'

'No?' he said tauntingly.

'If there is a reason, then tell me.'

He took a stride towards her, moved out of the shadows so that she could see his face now, his lips curled scornfully, as he said, 'I just wish I'd known you for what you are before yesterday. I wish to hell I hadn't degraded myself by going to bed with a slut who sleeps around the way you do!'

Appalled, her voice rose as Dyan cried out, 'How *dare* you call me that?'

She went to stride past him, overwhelmed by anger, but he stepped in front of her, barring the way. 'What's the matter; don't you like hearing the truth? Do you like it all wrapped up as a big romance? How many men have you told that you loved them? How many have you seduced into your bed? Flaunting yourself at them. Using your body and that beautiful face to drive them out of their senses, to make them forget everything else but wanting you. Well, how many is it? Or have you lost count, you slut?'

'Oh, God, how can you do this?' She tried to push past him. 'Get out of my way.'

But he wouldn't move, and smiled cruelly as he said, 'Oh, but I haven't even begun. I'm going to teach you just what decent people think of a scheming, dirty little cat like you.' Dyan gasped with shock and went to turn and run from him, but Oliver caught her arm and pulled her roughly round to face him. 'Oh, no, you don't. I haven't finished with you yet.'

'Let go of me or I'll scream!'

He laughed, a harsh mirthless sound. 'So that the crew will come to your rescue? Do you think I'm afraid of them? Do you think I care that you've already spread your poison, getting them on your side so that they ignore me?'

'I didn't! It was your own fault. You shouldn't have——'

Ignoring her protest, he said scathingly. 'Just how many of them have you been to bed with? All of them? The married men as well? Just for kicks. Does that excite you, having them——?'

'Shut up! Shut up!' Trying to pull away from him, close to tears, Dyan cried out, 'If you hate me so much why did you come back to the ship? Why didn't you just leave, for God's sake?'

But he shook her arm, his fingers digging into her flesh, for the first time using physical force on her. Looking into his eyes, she was appalled to see them blazing with malevolent fury. 'Because I'm going to teach you a lesson you're *never* going to forget.'

She gave a sob of despair and struggled to get free. 'No! Leave me alone. You have no right to do this to me.'

His face hardened cruelly and he easily dragged her back against him. 'Well, that's where you're wrong, you beautiful little bitch. Because I have every right to——'

There was the sound of running footsteps and the seaman on watch came hurrying up. He was carrying a torch and shone it on them. 'Let her go! You heard me; let her go or I'll smash your face in,' he shouted.

Oliver, quite unafraid, gave him a derisory look, and held her arm for a moment longer before dropping it as if it was something filthy he'd found in the gutter.

When the light had shone on her, Dyan had instinctively lifted her free hand to cover her face, not because the light had blinded her, but because she didn't want anyone to see how close she was to breaking down.

'You all right, boss? If he's hurt you——'

'What's happening? What's going on?' The first mate, alarmed by the noise, came hurrying towards them.

'It's nothing. I——'

But Dyan's voice was drowned out by the crewman's indignant, 'Balfour was attacking the boss. I saw him.'

The mate clenched his fists and faced up to Oliver. 'Oh, you were, were you, boyo?' he began menacingly.

'No, he wasn't,' Dyan cut in crossly, raising her voice to make herself heard. 'We were—were having an argument, that's all. About—about whether whale fishing should be banned or not,' she said, plucking an excuse out of the air.

She needn't have bothered because nobody believed her.

'Want to make something of it?' Oliver snarled, squaring up to the two sailors.

'No!' Dyan's voice was really angry now. She turned to the mate. 'Get back on the bridge where you belong. And you get back on patrol,' she ordered the crewman. 'When I want your help, I'll ask for it. Well, what are you waiting for?'

She stood still, her face implacable, and reluctantly they obeyed her, looking back to where she stood, waiting.

When they'd gone Oliver gave a harsh laugh. 'I can take care of myself. I don't need *you* to protect me.'

Dyan turned to face him, all other emotions buried beneath a cold, seething rage. 'Maybe you don't, but I won't have any fighting aboard this ship.' Her head came up. 'And if it comes to that I don't need any help to fight *my* battles, either. You don't scare me. Nobody as small-minded as you can scare me.'

Oliver's eyes narrowed, settled on her face. 'That almost sounds like a declaration of war.'

'You can take it any way you damn well like. And you can do and say what you damn well like. Because you can't hurt me, not any more.' She smiled, her green eyes as cold as glacier ice. 'Because I despise you for the warped, evil-minded coward that you are!'

And turning on her heel, she left him watching her as she strode away.

CHAPTER SIX

DYAN had never had to take sleeping pills in her life, but that night she would have resorted to them with intense gratitude. She slept little, her mind a mine-field of emotions, and when she got up in the morning had to use make-up to try and disguise the dark circles of sleeplessness around her eyes.

She went to the galley just as dawn was breaking, before even the cook was around, to make herself a mug of coffee which she took back to the ops room to drink. If skipping breakfast was ducking out, then it was just too bad, Dyan decided. There was no way she was going to face all the men this early in the day. By now, she knew, it would have gone all round the ship that she and Oliver had been quarrelling on the deck last night. Work served as an excuse, as she used their satellite communication to check on the latest weather conditions, and called the Hurricane Centre to make sure there wasn't the faintest breath of a hurricane anywhere within a thousand miles. 'No worries,' they assured her. 'The big winds haven't woken up from their winter hibernation yet.'

She also carefully measured the ocean current and then took all her information up to the bridge to wait for Russ to come up from the galley. He did so, a short time later, rubbing an unshaven chin. Raising an eyebrow when he saw her, he said, 'You're around early, Logan.'

'I'm eager to know if we've found the *Xanadu*,' she told him in half-truth.

'Better get going, then.'

Russ took over the bridge from the second mate and ordered the helmsman to return to the surface marker-buoy that they'd dropped over the wreck the previous evening. Only then did Dyan go down to the main deck to oversee the launch of the submersible. The divers and most of the crew, whether on watch or not, were already waiting there, interested to see what was going on.

As Dyan approached them she heard someone murmur, 'The boss is coming,' but took little notice. Now that she had a task on which she could concentrate, which would need all her attention, she was able to push everything else out of her mind, even Oliver, for a short while. She went to speak to the first mate, but he turned away as she came up and went to talk on the telephone to Russ, so Dyan turned instead to Hal and they discussed which divers would go down on this first dive.

'I'll go and I'll take Dave, the new man, with me. He hasn't been down in this particular type of submersible before. It will give me an opportunity to see how he gets on.'

'OK.' She gave him copies of her measurements of the current strength and the weather reports. 'It's really calm; you shouldn't have any trouble. Did you study the photographs of the boat we're looking for?' He nodded, as she'd known he would. 'Think you'll have much trouble recognising it?'

'No. It was pretty clear from the video pictures that...' He had glanced over her shoulder and his voice trailed off for a moment. 'That it must be the right one,' he finished, but still looking past her.

Puzzled, Dyan turned round and saw that Oliver had come up to join the other men. He was wearing jeans and a navy sweater against the early morning chill, his dark hair lifting in the breeze. He also had a skin graze on his right cheek and a band-aid that covered a cut over his right eye. Clear evidence that he had been in a fight. If there was contempt or any other kind of emotion in his eyes, Dyan didn't wait to see it. She whirled round to face the men, finding them all watching her, agog with curiosity to see what she might—or might not do, knowing that if she did nothing, said nothing, it would be giving tacit consent to what had been done, to what might be done in the future.

Her eyes searched the faces, saw who was missing, noticed, too, that the first mate was still standing by the phone with his back to her, the conversation going on over-long. Striding over to him she swung him round, not in the least surprised to see the large bruise over his eye that was already turning black.

'Who else?' she demanded furiously.

He shook his head. 'No one.'

Dyan didn't believe him for a second. 'Get them,' she ordered. 'And bring them to the ops room. *Now*!'

She didn't wait to see if he would obey her, just strode angrily to the ops room where she dismissed the crewman on duty and continued to pace up and down until the first mate came with two more sailors, one of them the man who had run to her rescue last night. Both of the sailors also had black eyes and looked a lot worse off than Oliver did. Even so, not bothering to hide her rage, letting them see how angry she was, Dyan said forcefully, 'Last night I gave you an order. I told you to leave Mr Balfour alone. And don't tell me he came seeking you out for a fight, because I won't believe it. You deliberately went against my orders and decided to teach him a lesson. Only it looks as if you three were the ones who were taught a lesson.'

They looked discomfited, and the officer opened his mouth to speak, but Dyan swept on, 'Well, now you're going to learn another lesson. Mr Balfour——' again using the surname to stress that he had special status '—is a customer of Starr Marine and a guest on this ship. He is to be treated with respect and politeness at all times. If I find that he has been attacked or treated discourteously in any way, then I shall have no hesitation in putting the person or people responsible ashore. Whatever their rank,' she added with an angry look at the mate. 'And I would also like you to remember,' she said, her voice sharpening, 'that I can handle my own problems. I don't need a dozen well-intentioned pseudo-champions doing it for me. Do I make myself clear?'

They nodded but Dyan continued to glower at them. 'As it is,' she said bitterly, 'you've now put me in the position of having to apologise to Balfour on your behalf.'

'We can do any apologising that's necessary,' the mate said gruffly.

She shook her head. 'No, he wouldn't accept it from you. All right, you can go. Send the man on watch back in.'

They went out, looking sheepish, but Dyan stayed there for a few moments, thinking that if she had allowed them to apologise to Oliver he wouldn't have believed them. He was bound to be convinced that she had set them on him, and only to have her personally apologise, to have her grovel, would stop him reporting the men and getting them dismissed from the ship, if not from Starr Marine. Two days ago she would have been certain that Oliver would never do such a thing, but now that she'd seen the other side of him, knew how vindictive he could be for little or no cause, she had no doubt that he would report the men. If he hadn't done so already. But when the crewman came back and she asked him if Oliver had been in the ops room to use the phone that morning he shook his head in denial. And he hadn't attempted to use the phone earlier when she'd been working there, so maybe there was a chance yet.

'If he comes in to use the phone, don't let him use it. Make some excuse or other. Then let me know immediately so that I can talk to him.'

The man nodded, obviously aware of the fight, and guessing her intentions. 'OK, boss.'

Outside in the corridor she hesitated, wondering if Oliver would be in his cabin, but somehow she didn't think so; it would be a matter of bravado with him to stay among the men on deck, his presence a challenge in itself. So her apology would have to wait. She walked back on deck, her hair tied in its usual plait, but with a long, loose sweater over her shirt and tight black Bermuda shorts over her long legs instead of her customary sawn-off denims. The men were still waiting and looked at her with interest, but she gave nothing away, instead giving orders for the submersible to be swung out over the fantail and launched.

Oliver was still there, too, just as she'd expected, but she took little notice of him until the submersible with its name, *Barney*, painted on it, was floating at the side of the deck and the men were getting into it. Then she went towards him and said, with the cool politeness of a society hostess to a not very welcome guest, 'This is a special kind of submersible, capable of lifting quite heavy weights, which might be necessary if we have to raise the safe separately. As you can see, it also has its own tiny unmanned submersible stowed in a cage at the front. We call it *Barney Junior*. This can be operated from inside the submersible to look at parts of the wreck that the larger vessel can't get to.'

Oliver's eyebrows had risen and his face had grown wary as she'd come up to him, but when she started to speak his face changed and a whole host of emotions showed fleetingly in his eyes: surprise, perhaps admiration, definite bleakness, comprehension; but then they hardened into cool mockery.

'Thank you for keeping me informed,' he said on a sardonic note.

She nodded and walked back to watch the entry hatch on the submersible being closed. Then it went through a whole series of tests while still on the surface to make sure that everything was working perfectly before it slowly sank beneath the waves.

Dyan turned again to where Oliver was standing alone, the men still avoiding him. 'Perhaps you would care to come down to the ops room with me and see their progress for yourself?'

He fell into step beside her as they walked back along the deck, but she lengthened her stride so that she entered the ship ahead of him. The corridor was empty, most of the men still on deck. Realising that she must take advantage of the opportunity, Dyan stopped and turned to face him. 'I must apologise to you on behalf of the men who attacked you,' she said, trying to keep her face and her voice as expressionless as possible. 'They have already been reprimanded and it won't happen again.'

'That must have cost you an effort. Who reprimanded them? You?'

'Yes.'

'Did Russ order you to do it?'

'No, of course not.'

'What's the matter, then; afraid of losing my company's future custom?'

Trying hard to control herself, Dyan answered, 'No. You're a guest on this ship.'

He laughed, then said in a disbelieving tone that was an insult in itself, 'What did you give the mate to get his gang together to try and beat me up—your body?'

She flinched, her eyes flashing fire, but managed to control her temper and didn't answer. She just turned away and went to walk along the narrow corridor, but Oliver caught her wrist and swung her round, then pushed her against the metal bulkhead and held her there as he loomed over her.

'I asked you a question, you beautiful little bitch!'

Dyan glared back at him, knowing that he couldn't physically hurt her, not here on the ship, and her emotions too numb to feel any further pain. 'No, you didn't. All you did was throw a cheap insult at me. Did it make you feel good?' she demanded contemptuously. 'Do you like talking dirty?'

His brows flickered and she thought he recoiled a little when he saw the way she looked at him, but then Oliver gave a snarling kind of grin. 'There's no other way to talk about you. You're the worst kind of slut—one who doesn't care who she goes after, or who she hurts in the process.' His voice was harsh and charged with emotion, as if she really had given him some cause for being so cruel.

Dyan frowned in utter perplexity, and made one last try. '*Why* do you keep saying that? What have I done to you?'

For a long moment he looked down into her unhappy green eyes. Again emotions chased through his face, but again his face hardened and his mouth twisted scornfully. 'What have you done to me?' His hands, gripping her wrists, tightened. 'Nothing like as much as I'm going to do to you. Now answer the question: was it your idea to beat me up?'

Seeing the anger in his face, the contempt in his eyes, the cruel twist to his mouth, and the determination in his out-thrust jaw, Dyan knew that he would only believe the worst of her whatever she said. If she told him it hadn't been her fault he wouldn't believe her anyway. Not that she would have done that; ultimately it had been her responsibility because the men hadn't obeyed her order to leave him alone. So, lifting her chin, she gave him what he wanted. 'Yes, it was,' she said with all the conviction she could muster. 'Entirely my idea. I got fed up with your pseudo-macho strong-arm tactics, so I decided to teach you a lesson. You're ready enough to use brute force with me, with a woman, so I thought I'd let you see what it was like to stand up to a man for a change.'

'One man?'

She smiled at him sweetly. 'Two to stop you when you ran away, like the coward you are.'

'Only I didn't run, and it was they who got the lesson.' It was his turn to smile. 'I told you I could take care of myself; you should have believed me.'

'So I should.' She gave him a baleful look. 'Which means that you're just a sadistic pervert who enjoys hurting women.'

The smile fled from his face. 'I'm no sadist,' he said harshly.

'Then let me go.'

Oliver looked at her for a moment. He let go of one of her hands and she thought that he was going to release her, but then he gave a small laugh. 'Nice try. But you're in a different category altogether. You don't count as a woman. You're just a cheap little slut. A tease. But you like sex—that I do know. Don't you?' And lifting his hand he put it inside her sweater and began to caress her breast.

Immediately her hand came up to strike him, but he saw it coming, had been expecting it, and swiftly caught her wrist with his other hand, holding both of them in his fist, so that he could caress her as he willed, laughing mockingly as he did so.

For a second, before she could control it, a great tremor of desire ran through her. He felt it, damn him, and gave a laugh of cruel pleasure. Gritting her teeth, Dyan braced herself to knee him, and was about to do so when she heard her name being called over the tannoy. Their eyes met, then Oliver laughed again before he let her go and backed off.

'Next time,' he said in derisive threat. 'Next time.'

Without looking at him, Dyan strode away, but her shoulders were back and there was defiance in every inch of her tall, slim body.

'Sorry. Got held up,' she apologised hurriedly as she entered the ops room.

Taking her seat in front of the screens, she contacted the submersible. Hal's voice, remarkably clear, came over the intercom. 'Hello, boss, thought you'd abandoned us.'

'I thought of it, but the company wants its sub back,' she managed to joke. 'Are all your underwater tests OK?'

'Sure. Everything's fine.'

Dyan glanced at the reading on the desk in front of her that gave the submersible's depth. 'OK, take her down to five hundred feet and check again.'

She took the craft gradually down to the sea-bed and it began to send back film of the wreck, the cameras zooming in to take close-up shots. Oliver, she knew, had followed her into the room, but she was able to ignore him now as she talked to Hal.

'The bow of the boat is partially covered,' he reported. 'I'm going to try and blow the sand off so that hopefully we'll be able to read her name.'

For several minutes the camera showed only a cloud of sand as the air-jets sent it swirling up into the sea, then it slowly settled until they could again see the bow of the sunken boat. And now the name showed clearly. *Xanadu*. Around her the men who had come to watch gave shouts of triumph and punched the air.

'Nice one, Logan,' Russ said behind her.

'It's like a pin-prick in the chart of the ocean,' someone else commented. 'But she always finds it.'

Dyan raised her own hand in acknowledgement, but concentrated on the screen. 'Can you see if the boat's intact, Hal? I particularly want to know if the safe has fallen out of her.'

'Can't see any extensive damage. Do you want me to send *Junior* in to take a look?'

The little robot, controlled from the submersible, was set free and began its exploration of the *Xanadu*. It felt uncanny watching the images it sent to the screen, its brilliant light sending a clear picture to those watching above. It was rather like a person walking over the deck and into a ghost ship. Which was what it was, really, except that there were no dead bodies on this craft. The robot went into a cabin and they saw the circular bed, the once luxurious fittings of dressing-table and wardrobes, the clothes still on their hangars and moving as if being selected by an invisible hand.

'Good grief!' The quiet, amazed exclamation came from behind her and she recognised Oliver's voice.

Glancing round she saw his gaze riveted on one of the screens above his head. His profile was sharp, his hair still dishevelled from the breeze outside. Another intense wave of feeling encompassed her, making her heart swell in her chest, but this time it was of love, the purest love. Oliver must have felt her eyes on him, because he looked quickly down, catching her before she could turn away. Seeing the infinite sadness in her face, he became very still, and went on staring at her for a long moment after she had turned away.

Her voice a little husky, Dyan instructed Hal to send the robot further into the boat, to where the safe was located. It continued on its eerie way and found the safe still in position and apparently intact.

'Well done,' Dyan told them. 'OK, that's enough for this time. Come on up.'

The rest of the day was taken up with work: developing the camera film of still shots taken by the two submersibles, going carefully through them and the video films of the *Xanadu* again, checking its tonnage plus that of the safe, and then working out whether it would be possible to lift the boat intact or whether they would have to break it up and take the safe out separately. Towards the end of the afternoon, she got through to Oliver on the ship's intercom phone and asked him to come to the ops room. But this time she made sure that the crewman on duty at the radar screen stayed at his post.

Oliver glanced at him when he came in, and when Dyan didn't dismiss him, gave a small smile as if amused by her tactics.

Getting straight down to business, Dyan said, 'I've studied the film and the photographs we've taken of the *Xanadu*, and I want to tell you the options open to us.' She gestured to the black and white photos laid out on the table and Oliver came over to look at them. 'As you can see, the boat's hull appears to be in pretty good condition. All I can see is a hole just above the sand line. Here.' She indicated the point on one of the shots with a pencil.

Oliver picked up the photo to look at it more closely, then gave her a quick glance. 'It's very difficult to tell. It could be just a shadow.'

'It's not,' she said with certainty.

'What makes you so sure?'

'Experience,' she said crisply.

Another brief smile, but this time of amusement, came to his lips but was quickly gone as Oliver's jaw tightened and his eyes grew cold. 'Very well. Knowing you to be a woman of vast experience, I'll take your word for it.' There was the smallest note of sarcasm in his tone when he said 'vast', a nuance that she picked up at once. She gave him a derisive look that said more clearly than words, So you can't even keep your evil-mindedness out of business!

The crewman stirred and she saw his back stiffen; so he must have heard it, too. She sighed inwardly, knowing it would give rise to more gossip, and someone was bound to think that there was no smoke without fire. So far, she knew, most of the crew, those who'd sailed with her before, were fiercely partisan on her behalf. But the new men were bound to wonder just what she'd done to upset Oliver so badly, and if he made more remarks like that they might well think it was because he'd found out that she was promiscuous or something. If not worse. Dyan had few illusions about the way rumours could spread and grow in the narrow confines of a ship.

Ignoring his remark, she said, 'These are our options: one, we can patch up the boat's hull and try to raise it with the safe still in her. Two, we can rip out the safe and forget the boat—that would be far the quickest. Or three——' she pointed to a plan of the *Xanadu* '—we can take out the ceiling of the main cabin, here, plus the floor below it, lift the safe out of the hole, and then lift the boat.'

Oliver leaned an elbow on the high chart table and bent to take a closer look at the plan. His eyes became engrossed and she had a glimpse of his professional persona: the successful business executive rather than the lover—and the hater.

'Would the boat itself be worth anything after being in the water all this time? Could it be restored to anything like its former condition?'

'Oh, yes. It's a good boat by a good maker. You could either sell it as it is for restoration or you could have the work done and then sell it.'

'But would any buyer trust it after it sank?'

'I don't see why not. It was the combination of the heavy safe and the hurricane that sank it, not anything wrong with the boat itself.'

'It would have been better if the makers had refused to install the safe at all,' Oliver commented. 'They must have known it would make the vessel unseaworthy.'

'They didn't put it in. Your pop star had the safe-makers put it in. They weren't to know about the importance of distribution of weight ratios in a seagoing vessel, how it would react in a hurricane.'

'The captain should have done.'

'Yes,' Dyan admitted. But added in quick defence of the unknown seaman, 'But it sailed over to Europe OK. It was only when the owner started filling the safe that the imbalance probably started. You've read the list of the things that were in it; there were several heavy bronzes and even a couple of stone statues. It really needed a much bigger boat to take all that.'

'So which of these options do you recommend?'

'The first one, lifting the whole thing, will take the longest. Two weeks at least, possibly more.' She didn't say it, but it was heavy in the air that to spend another two weeks with him on the ship would be traumatic in the least. 'As I said, the second option would be the quickest. If we smashed open the *Xanadu* and hauled out the safe we could do it within three days maximum. The third option would take longer and would mean more renovation work, but the glass windows of the main cabin are already broken and the ceiling buckled where the boat must have landed partly on its roof and then rolled over on the sea-bed. To take out the ceiling and floor wouldn't take more than a couple of days, but it would be tricky manoeuvring the safe through the hole without doing any damage to the boat. But when that was done it wouldn't be difficult to raise the wreck once it was lightened of the weight of the safe. Say about ten days.'

Oliver straightened, considered. 'I'm dismissing the second option unless the other two fail,' he said decisively. 'We'll save the boat if we can. And we'll try the first option first. Lift the whole thing.'

He was looking at her, but Dyan kept her eyes averted as she gathered up the photos. 'Against that, of course,' she pointed out, 'you have to weigh the cost of this operation, of the salvage vessel.'

'I have weighed the cost,' he answered, but not talking about the salvage. 'It's one I'm quite happy to accept.'

His eyes were on her still, and now she felt compelled to look at him, but was unsurprised by the malevolence in his eyes. 'The *Xanadu* must have been an expensive boat,' she remarked, meeting his eyes but refusing to rise to the bait.

'It was. I understand it cost well over a million pounds to build and fit out. Worth another couple of weeks, don't you think?'

'The choice is yours,' she said shortly. 'As is the responsibility.'

'Oh, no,' he said with silky menace, making his meaning clear. 'The responsibility is yours and the results of your actions are also entirely on your own head.'

She gazed into his eyes, grey and menacing as a snow cloud, then her chin came up in open defiance and, to his surprise, she gave a short laugh. 'OK, if that's the way you want it.'

'That's right,' Oliver commented, and raised his voice slightly as he added, for the crewman's benefit, 'Never argue with a paying customer.'

Her cheeks flushed, knowing what he'd meant to imply. Quickly she said, 'Yes, your company is paying Starr Marine,' but she knew that it was too late; that remark, too, would be reported and there was bound to be speculation that she had sold herself to him. Curtly she said, 'Now that you've made your decision I needn't keep you. I'm sure you'll want to go and socialise with the crew over a drink before dinner,' she added sarcastically, knowing that all the men were still avoiding him like the plague.

He merely gave her a derisive grin, but at least he left without saying anything more. Thinking about him was like an emotional minefield, but talking to him was like being shot at by a line of accurate snipers, Dyan thought as she went into the office to call Barney and tell him of Oliver's decision.

'How's it going, Logan?' Barney asked her afterwards.

'Oh, just fine,' she lied.

'You still getting on OK with Balfour?'

'Oh, sure, but now he's decided what he wants us to do we don't really need him any more. If you let his company know maybe they'd be glad to recall him.'

'The arrangement was for him to stay until the wreck was safely recovered. Balfour should know whether he has anything more to do there or not. What's the matter; he looking over your shoulder too much?'

'Something like that,' she admitted.

Barney laughed. 'Dealing with customers is all part of the job. You know that. You'll just have to learn to handle him, Logan. Any other problems?'

'No; the submersible and its robot are working fine.'

'I hear you gave 'em a name.'

'Oh, really?' she said innocently, trying to hide the laughter in her voice.

'Yeah, my name.'

'How did you find out?' she asked indignantly.

'I got spies everywhere,' he chuckled. 'So long, Logan. Good luck with the lift.'

She put down the phone, wondering if he really did have someone on the ship who reported to him. Russ, probably. But would Russ tell him about the situation that had arisen between her and Oliver? Probably, she thought again with dismal fatalism. The two were old sea-dogs from way back, had often sailed together, and she wasn't at all sure that Russ's fondness for herself would outweigh his loyalty to Barney. If he thought that there was something Barney ought to know, something important to the running of the ship, then he would tell him. Which meant that her job would be on the line.

Momentarily overcome by the anguish of it all, Dyan rested her head on her hand, thinking that if this was what falling in love did to you, then she was surprised the human race hadn't come to a standstill centuries ago. But it was only for a moment, then her natural fighting spirit came to her rescue. She had worked extremely hard for years to get to where she was now, and she was darned if she was going to let a perverted pig like Oliver take it away from her. She would just make absolutely sure that the lift went perfectly, so Barney would have no real reason to sack her.

Unless he blamed her for the men ganging up to attack Oliver. Unless Oliver kicked up a stink and used his company, threatening not to give Barney any more work unless she was sacked.

Torn between pessimism and fight, Dyan went to her cabin to shower and change before dinner, but now had little interest in clothes and merely put on a clean pair of jeans and a sweater. The men were still protecting her, still ostracising Oliver, and tonight she took advantage of it, sitting well away from him, both during dinner and afterwards in the rest room. But she merely picked at her food and couldn't concentrate on the film they were all watching on the video. When it was over she stood up and wished everyone a general goodnight.

Hal also got to his feet. 'Think I'll turn in myself. I guess we'll be starting at first light tomorrow, won't we, boss?'

He fell in beside her as she walked along to her cabin, chatting about the morrow.

When they reached her door she turned to him. 'Do you really think I need an escort?' she asked wryly.

'Why is he doing this to you?' Hal demanded. 'I thought you and he were—well...'

'I don't know,' she admitted tiredly. 'I just don't know, Hal.' Tears pricked at her eyes and she said hurriedly, 'Well, goodnight. Thanks for—for being kind.' And she went quickly into her cabin.

Dyan was so tired that she thought she would fall instantly asleep, but as soon as her head touched the pillow her stupid brain kept on going over that nasty incident with Oliver this morning, and over every glance they'd exchanged, every double-meaning remark he'd made since. But mostly her mind kept coming back to that moment when she had known that, no matter what he'd done to her in the last couple of days, she loved him still. Which was a damn fool way to feel. Miserably she wondered why it was that she always made unerringly for the wrong man, why she couldn't have fallen in love with some nice, safe, ordinary guy. Someone who would love her in return and could always be relied on not to go off the rails, not to hurt her and treat her like dirt. There were men all around her, most of them unmarried; why couldn't she have fallen for one of them instead of a louse like Oliver?

The next morning she was up early to watch over the first dive. Tired-eyed, head aching, but there. Oliver came on deck to watch as the submersible went over the side and followed her down to the ops room, but this time she took good care that she had someone with her, just as she made sure that she was never alone with him for the rest of the day.

The submersible went down twice that day, the first time to clear the sand from the hole in the hull that Dyan had seen, the second time to fix a watertight patch over it. For this second operation they had to use the little robot and it was slow and tricky, but they had the patch firmly in place by the end of the afternoon. Dyan called a halt to work for the day and she was about to leave the ops room when the man at the radar screen called out, 'We've got company, boss.'

Quickly she crossed to look, saw a blip that was getting nearer. Several craft had passed them at the periphery of the screen during the last two days, but, because they were off the shipping lanes, no one had come near them. This ship, though, seemed to be coming directly towards them. 'Tell Russ,' she ordered, and picking up a pair of binoculars ran up to the bridge.

He already had his glasses to his eyes and was studying the ship that was gradually coming nearer.

'What do you make of her?' Dyan asked.

'She's flying a Panamanian flag. Looks like a cargo boat.'

'She's way off course, if she is.'

'Mm.' The phone rang and Russ went to answer it. He listened, then said to Dyan, 'They're asking if we need assistance. Said as we weren't moving they thought we might be in difficulties.'

Dyan gave a disbelieving laugh. 'Unfortunately they'll have seen the submersible being brought back on board.' She thought for a minute. 'Thank them for their offer, but tell them we're just doing an oceanography survey on the effects of bright light on the larvae of deep sea eels and echiuroid worms.'

Russ rolled his eyes, but spoke into the phone, passing on her message. Afterwards he picked up his glasses again, and said, 'Are there such things?'

'Yes, of course.'

He grinned at her. 'Well, I hope I'm not around if they ever really do a survey on them.'

Dyan smiled in return and went to turn away, but Russ said roughly, 'You look terrible, Logan. You sure you can handle this? I can turn the ship round and put Balfour ashore, you know, whether he likes it or not.'

She put a grateful hand on his arm, but shook her head. 'No, I'm OK. Of course I am,' she said valiantly.

That evening she again took good care to keep away from Oliver, and he made no move to get near her, although his eyes met hers once or twice in amused derision. But she could cope with that, could cope with almost anything except his snarling insults and open contempt.

Again she went to bed early; the first mate this time stood in the corridor between her cabin and the galley to make sure that Oliver didn't follow her, and gave her a cheery wave goodnight when she reached her door. But again Dyan couldn't sleep.

Angrily she turned on her side, thumping the pillow, and determinedly closing her eyes, desperate for sleep, trying to shut it all out. But it was no use, she was still awake in the early hours of the morning, and by now her head was aching so much that she knew she'd *never* get to sleep. Turning on the light, she got out of bed and searched in her drawer, then the bathroom cabinet for some headache pills. Finding the packet, she opened it eagerly, then threw it down on the ground in disgust. Empty! Only then did she remember that she'd taken the last two that morning to help her recover from last night's hours of sleeplessness. 'Damn, damn, damn!' she swore, knowing that she would have to go to the first-aid box in the galley to get some more.

At night she wore only a pair of short cotton pyjamas, but they covered her adequately enough so she didn't bother to put anything else on as she quietly opened her door and padded, bare-footed, to the galley. There were lights burning in the corridors, dim reddish bulbs that were always on at night in case of emergency. Already light-headed through lack of sleep, it created an eerie atmosphere to Dyan's tired mind, the long corridor stretching out like some endless path in a nightmare. Russ's cabin wasn't along this corridor, he had a suite under the bridge, but Oliver's and all the other officers' cabins were along here.

The first-aid box was in a cupboard just inside the door to the galley. Dyan turned on the light and found a large bottle of aspirins. She shook several out into her hand and put most of them into the pocket of her pyjama jacket, saving two to take. There was a big American fridge-freezer in the galley that had a chilled water facility. Dyan poured some into a glass and took the pills, afterwards taking a long drink of the cool water. It felt so good she got some more and poured it over her wrists at the sink, letting it trickle over the fine blue veins. Perhaps a cold shower would help her to sleep, she thought, but no; that would only make her more awake. Dyan dried her hands and switched off the light, walked quietly back to her cabin.

As she reached it she thought she heard the click of a door behind her, and she looked back, ready to apologise if she'd disturbed anyone, but there was no one there. Putting it down to imagination, Dyan went into her cabin and sat down on the edge of her bed for a moment. The door opened and Oliver came in. He shut the door, locked it, and put the key in the

pocket of the shorts he was wearing. Smiling unpleasantly, he said, 'As you seem to be making
yourself available to all the men tonight, I thought I
might as well have my turn.'

CHAPTER SEVEN

THE shock was so great that it was a moment before Dyan could react. Then she lunged for the phone, but Oliver strode over and covered her hand before she could pick up the receiver. 'Go ahead,' he said curtly. 'But I'll tell anyone who comes that you invited me here.'

She stared at him for a moment, but then drew her hand away, making no further attempt to make the call. 'That's exactly the kind of lie I'd expect you to tell,' she said jeeringly.

'They say that people get what they deserve,' Oliver pointed out.

'There can be very few people who would deserve you!'

'Ah, but you're a special case.' He put a hand under her chin, forcing her head back as he looked down into her face. His own features were hard and set, but as she glared up at him, Dyan saw a muscle work at the corner of his mouth and a strangely bleak look fill his eyes. 'I'll never know how someone who looks the way you do can be so vile inside.'

'Don't you?' she retaliated. 'Why don't you look in the mirror?'

That made his fingers tighten and the usual look of contempt come back into his eyes. 'Whose bed have you come from?'

'I went to the galley to get some aspirins. I have a headache.'

He laughed unpleasantly. 'Do you really expect me to believe such a half-baked excuse?'

'No, of course not. I expect you to go on getting cheap kicks by treating me like dirt.' Her eyes filled with scorn. 'Is that what turns you on? Is that what gives you your perverted pleasure? Making girls fall for you enough to go to bed with you, then turning on them, humiliating and degrading them, just because they were stupid enough to——?'

'No!' The curt negative cut her short. 'I'm no pervert. And if there's any humiliation, any stupidity in this, then it was mine. For allowing myself to fall for a lying, heartless woman like you. When I found out what you were...' His hand slid to her throat, tightened. 'I could have killed you. For making such a fool of me. For destroying all my——' Again the bleak look came into his eyes and he broke off abruptly. Then said, 'That was when I decided I was going to make you pay for all the harm you've done. To me. And to mine.'

'Yours?' She said the word with difficulty because he was still holding her throat.

'Yes, mine.' He looked at her, let his gaze slide down her body. 'And that's why I came here tonight. Who were you with?' he demanded again. She didn't answer, but it seemed that he didn't really expect her to. His eyes growing intent, Oliver let his hand slip down from her throat, quite slowly, to the neck of her pyjamas.

Instantly, she jerked away, tried to reach for the phone again. But Oliver pushed her back on the bed and came down on top of her, pinning her back with his body. Dyan flailed at him with her fists and tried to scream, but he put his hand over her mouth, silencing her.

He laughed softly and for a few moments looked down at her, enjoying the helpless anger that blazed in her eyes, enjoying his power over her. Then Oliver said mockingly, 'Why pretend, Dyan? You know that it doesn't matter what I do to you; you still want me. You had a good time, that night we spent together. And that's what your body craves, doesn't it—a good time? Sexual satisfaction?' Bending, he took his hand from her mouth, but before she could cry out, replaced it with his own mouth. His lips were hard, there was no hint of tenderness, not even desire. But they were a sensuous, erotic reminder of that night of love. Even though the object of his kiss was to mock and degrade her, Dyan couldn't help but be instantly transported back to that night.

Because she realised her vulnerability, she tried to fight him, turning her head away and when he brought her back, trying to bite him. But he laughed against her mouth and forced her lips open, whispering, 'But this is what you like, Dyan. This is what you want.'

'No! Get out. Leave me alone.'

Lifting his head, Oliver put his hands on either side of her face. Looking down at her, his expression was for the moment unreadable, as he said, 'Beg me to go, then.'

She stared at him, wondering if this was to be her final humiliation, that he needed to hear her grovel and plead before he would be satisfied. But she hadn't invited him here and there was too much pride in her ever to beg, especially in these circumstances. So her lip curled as she said, 'I wouldn't beg from you. Never!'

'No?' His eyebrows rose. 'I wonder.' Again he bent to kiss her, still holding her down with his weight, but he lowered his right hand and began to undo the buttons of her pyjamas, doing each button slowly and deliberately.

Dyan bucked and tried to struggle, but he was far too strong for her. She swore at him and made protesting sounds against his mouth, furious at her own helplessness. But then his hand was on her skin, his fingers running gently over the curve of her breast, finding the soft bud of her nipple and stroking it into life.

'No!' Dyan moaned the sound out on a note of despair, but he continued to toy with her, arousing her senses against her will. No matter how she strove to control it, waves of frustrated sensuality coursed through her veins, awoke a fierce need deep inside her. Her head still beat with a dull ache and she felt dizzy with tiredness, unable to fight the pulsing heat, the aching need, the desperate *yearning* for love. And when Oliver took his mouth from hers and lowered it to kiss her breast she found that she couldn't scream, couldn't cry out for help as she knew, dimly in her mind, that she ought to do.

She gave a soft moan, the body that had known such wonderful lovemaking with him, betraying her completely. 'So, do you still want me to go?' he said against her ear.

She didn't answer, just looked at him with eyes full of desire, her lips parted for his kiss as he took her mouth again, exploring its inner moistness with his tongue.

Oliver rolled on to his side on the bed, sure of her now, and took off her jacket, throwing it on the floor so that the rest of the aspirins rolled out of her pocket. For a while he played with her breasts, kissing and toying with the nipples, making her gasp and writhe. Then he reached out and drew down the bottom half of her pyjamas, the soft material pulled slowly down her legs until it was entirely free and he tossed it aside.

He stroked her length with his hand and it was wonderful, wonderful, so soothing and yet so exciting. His hand went to her inner thigh, pushed her legs a little apart. For a moment, then, she resisted him, but his caressing fingers sent a great shudder of sensuousness through her, and with a long sigh of surrender she exposed herself to his gaze, to his touch.

During the night they had spent together, Dyan had learnt the joy and wonder of shared sexual fulfilment, now she learnt the exquisite delights that just a featherlight caress of the fingers could give. She gave little gasps and sighs of pleasure, all resistance lost beneath the knowing exploration, the experienced touch of his hands and lips. He stimulated and aroused her as never before, but when her hand went to his trousers so that she could give him his share of pleasure, Oliver stopped her. 'No.'

'But why?' She opened eyes heavy with sensual pleasure, with desire, to look at him, but immediately he started to caress her again, more deliberately now, and Dyan had to shut her eyes as she gave a shuddering cry of excitement. But frustration was growing now; she wanted him, wanted to run her hands over his naked body, feel his closeness. His touch was exciting but it wasn't enough. But he knew that, knew and encouraged it as she arched towards him, her body reacting to a basic instinct as old as time itself.

'Do you want me? Do you?' His voice was so thick, so unsteady, that the words came out in not much more than a whisper.

'Oh, yes. Oh, God, *yes*,' she answered in unhesitating urgency, everything else forgotten.

'Then say it. I want you to say it.'

She had to drag her eyes open, her arousal complete. Slowly she smiled, and lifted a hand to touch his face. 'I love you,' she said with deep sincerity.

His hand was on her waist and it immediately tightened. 'That wasn't what I asked,' Oliver said, his voice becoming rough. 'Tell me you want me.'

'Of course I want you.'

'Say please.'

Dyan blinked, hazily aware that this wasn't going right, but she was too excited and too tired to think about it, so obediently said, 'Please make love to me, my darling.'

He stood up, put his hand on her shoulder and shook her roughly. 'Open your eyes. Look at me.'

Reluctantly she did so, became aware that the light was on, that he still had all his clothes on. But it was the light of scornful triumph in his eyes that brought her back to cold reality with shocking clarity. She sat up, realised her nakedness and brought her knees together, put her arms across her chest in a gesture that was far too late.

Oliver laughed, reached out and put a hand under her chin, forcing her head up, not caring that he hurt her. 'You wouldn't beg me to leave, but you certainly begged me to take you.' Looking down at her, his eyes filled with loathing. 'You dirty little cat! Do you really think that I'd take other men's leavings?' Suddenly he pushed her away so that she fell back against the pillows. Turning, he walked to the door, looked back at her with that hateful smile on his face. She closed her eyes, unable to bear it, and didn't see Oliver, as he unlocked the door, notice something on the floor and frown for a moment before he went out, letting the door slam shut behind him.

When he'd gone, Dyan gazed into space with stunned eyes, then curled herself into a ball and for the first time cried herself to sleep.

The telephone ringing by her bed hauled Dyan into semi-wakefulness the next morning. 'Yes?'

'You getting up this morning, Logan?' Russ's voice demanded.

She peered at the alarm clock, moaned, and said, 'I'll be right there.'

The crew cheered good-naturedly when she appeared on deck ten minutes later, in jeans and a sweater, her hair still loose, and dark glasses covering her eyes. Dyan managed to find a grin for them, but then got straight down to work. They did two dives that day, the divers being changed because of the intense concentration needed to work the manipulator arms of the submersible. Some salvage bosses, she knew, would have kept the divers down there all day without a break to save money, but Dyan thought that all wrong. Most of the day she spent in the ops room, having a sandwich there instead of going into the galley for lunch. The divers were putting airbags into the *Xanadu* now, ready to fill them to help with the lift when the time came. It was routine work and she could have left someone else to oversee it, but Dyan never delegated responsibility when the divers were down.

She spent the evening in the ops room as well, talking on the phone to Barney to report progress, looking at the video film of the work done that day, working out what they would need to do tomorrow. The work was finished long before the evening was over, but Dyan stayed where she was. If Oliver thought she was hiding away from him and was gloating in the fact, then it was just too bad; until her eyes had lost their puffiness, until her beaten spirit had recovered a little, then the victory, if such he thought it, was his.

Around ten o'clock Dyan became aware that the ship was rolling more than usual. Looking at the barometer, she saw that it was falling, so she radioed for the latest weather reports and found that the wind was increasing, expected to be as strong as thirty to thirty-five knots during the night; apart from the storm, the strongest weather they'd had on the trip. Calling up Russ, she told him, and said, 'I'm not sending the sub down tomorrow if the wind is more than twenty knots. We'll just have to lose a day.'

'OK, Logan. You all right? Haven't seen you tonight.'

'Yes, fine,' she lied glibly. 'I'm doing some research on that old wreck we found last week.'

The wind was still high when she went to her cabin that night. Joe, the steward, hadn't been in to clean it today and the aspirins were still lying on the floor from last night, but two of them, she noticed, had been crushed underfoot. She frowned as she bent to clear them up, then realised that it must have been Oliver who had trodden on them last night. Depressed beyond belief, she expected to lie awake all night again but she fell asleep almost at once, and when she woke in the morning she felt the ship rolling in the swell and knew that there would be no diving that day, so she just turned over and went back to sleep again.

She slept the whole morning and past lunch time, and finally woke feeling more refreshed than she had since Oliver had first turned against her. But even then she didn't get up immediately, instead lying in deep thought, resolved to come to terms with this, and better able now to think it all through. Her life was in ruins for the second time, and again because of a man. But last time there had been a reason, and now that she was thinking more clearly, Dyan began to realise that there must be a reason now, too. There had been things Oliver had said, odd remarks he'd let drop but had refused to enlarge on. Looking back on them, Dyan became ever more sure that there had to be an explanation for his behaviour. And for her own peace of mind she had to know that reason. Even if she was wrong and it was just a perverted sense of cruelty, then she had to know.

But how to find out was going to be difficult, she realised. It seemed to be part of Oliver's cruelty not to tell her the reason, to leave her guessing in a game of cat and mouse. So she would have to think of some way in which she could coerce him into telling her. Which would mean getting him alone. That brought her up short, not at all willing to have to face his insults again. But the need to know was greater than her fear of him. If she was ever going to have any confidence in herself as a person again, then she had to find out why, if there was a reason, he had turned against her. And Oliver couldn't insult or humiliate her more than he had done. She had reached the depths, and the only way now was up.

When she had broken off her last romance Dyan had been heart-sick and unhappy, but now, after this physical rejection of her by Oliver, she withdrew into herself. Outwardly she did her work as thoroughly as ever, and in the evenings spent time in the rest room with the crew, watching videos and even playing poker, but she had lost the spontaneity and the open trust-fulness that was a great part of her warm and friendly personality. She didn't try to avoid Oliver any more, which must have puzzled him, because once or twice she caught him watching her with a frown between his eyes. And he must have decided that his victory was won, that he'd completely degraded her, because he made no further attempts to try and get her alone.

For over a week they worked on getting the cradle of slings under the *Xanadu*, ready to lift it, only to find that there was another hole, previously hidden by the sand, that had to be patched up first.

During the first few days, Dyan had been looking for a way to get Oliver alone. She could have asked him to see her in the ops room, of course, but she didn't want to do that, didn't want him to be on his guard or somewhere where he could just walk away if he didn't want to answer her. But now she'd thought of a way and patiently bided her time until she could bring it about.

Her only problem during that week was that Dave, the new diver and new to Starr Marine, had started to chat her up. Dyan hardly noticed at first, too en-grossed with her own problems to bother much about who talked to her and who didn't. It was only when she overheard one of the crew make a comment about it that she became aware that Dave was seeking her out too much, using the excuse of asking her about

other possibilities for diving in experimental oceanography, searching for underwater hot springs and
that kind of thing. Once she'd realised, Dyan took
care to avoid him or always be with other people when
he was around. But it was annoying because it gave
Oliver reason to sneer at her disdainfully again, and
she didn't want that, she wanted him to think her
completely cowed so that he wouldn't refuse to be
alone with her when the time came.

At last they were ready to try to lift the *Xanadu*.
The last sling was in place, the last cable attached,
the lifting gear checked. Hal brought the submersible
to the surface quite early in the morning to report this
to her, and Dyan turned to Oliver, who formed one
of the small crowd of people on deck who were waiting
for the sub to come up.

'As your company's representative, I expect that
you'd like to go down and see for yourself that we've
made all the correct preparations, left nothing to
chance?'

Oliver looked surprised. 'You want me to go down?'

'It's usual.' She shrugged. 'But you've seen all the
videos, so if you'd rather not of course——'

'On the contrary,' he interrupted, 'I'd very much
like to take the opportunity.'

To make sure that he'd accept, she again tried to
dissuade him, saying, 'Of course it's a long way down,
so if you're at all nervous it's quite understandable.'

'I'm not nervous,' Oliver said shortly. 'When shall
I go down?'

Dyan glanced at Hal. 'About twenty minutes?' she
questioned.

Hal nodded. 'You'll need a sweater,' he told Oliver.

Oliver left to fetch one from his cabin and Hal raised his eyebrows. 'Why do you want him to go down in the sub? We've never done it before.'

'I have a good reason.'

'You trying to give him a fright or something, boss? Because I can tell you now it won't work. Oliver isn't the type to be scared; he'll enjoy it.'

'No. I want to get him alone.'

'You mean *you're* going to take him down?'

'Yes.'

Hal looked startled, but didn't argue. Nor did he say anything when Oliver came back. They'd done the checks on the submersible and it was ready to go down again.

'You'll have to get in first and sit in the back seat,' Hal told him.

Oliver went to obey him, climbed halfway into the hatch, then glanced at Dyan as she stood nearby, watching. He paused, and said, 'Have you got something cooked up for me, Dyan?'

She gave him a curled-lip smile. 'Getting cold feet?' And added before he could speak, 'Don't go if you're afraid.'

Giving her a cold smile in return, Oliver dropped into the submersible. Hal leaned in to check that he was safely in his seat with the strap on, then turned to look expectantly at Dyan.

'Take control in the ops room,' she said to him, then dropped through the hatch and directly into the front seat, immediately reaching up to close the hatch above her.

'So that's it,' Oliver said behind her. He put a hand on her shoulder. 'So what's the big idea?'

Turning to look at him over her shoulder, she said tauntingly, 'Afraid?'

For a long moment he stared into her eyes, then let her go and sat back. 'Take her down,' he said shortly.

Dyan put on the headset. 'OK. Lower away,' she ordered.

The crane on the mother ship hoisted the submersible off the deck and lowered it into the sea. Dyan spoke on the radio to the ops room. 'Oxygen is running. Scrubber is on. Permission to dive.'

The answer came crackling through the earphones. 'Clear to dive when ready.'

The ballast tanks began to fill with water and they started to sink. At first it was light outside, the sunlight permeating down through the water, but then the light faded and it became absolutely black. There was a light inside the sub that cast a faint white glow into the surrounding sea. Particles of detritus drifting down from the surface seemed to race upwards past the window, giving the illusion that they were descending very fast, almost out of control. Dyan had seen the phenomenon many times, had known it would happen. But to Oliver it was new and startling. She heard him catch his breath, waited for him to tell her to slow down, or to stop and take him back to the surface. But he did neither of those things.

After a few minutes she turned on the running lights and he was able to see the illusion for what it was.

'Just how fast are we going down?' he asked wryly.

'Quite slowly—only about thirty metres per minute,' she admitted with grudging respect.

She expected him to ask her if she was competent to handle a sub, but he didn't, instead turning to look out of the window at a large fish that drifted over to take a look at them. Then a whole shoal of tiny, bright lights seemed to engulf them.

'What is it?' he asked on a gasp, but there was only amazement in his tone, not fear.

'They're krill; phosphorescent shrimps.'

He laughed. 'It's like the parade of a million lights at Disney World. How far down do we go?'

'About eight hundred metres.'

'Is that very deep for a vessel like this?'

'No. A naval submarine can go down to nine hundred metres. A man in a diving suit can go down to about six hundred metres. The bottom here is fairly shallow when you compare it to one of the deep trenches in the ocean.'

'What's the deepest part of the ocean?'

'Probably the Challenger Deep in the Pacific. Near the island of Guam. That goes down about eleven kilometres, but it has only been explored down to six thousand metres. Below that is the hadal zone.'

'The "hadal zone"?' Oliver queried.

'It's another name for the depths of hell.'

There was a short silence as they continued to descend, trailing their power cord and fibre-optic cable behind them. Then Oliver said, 'If people knew how wonderful this was they'd all want to come down here.'

'It's already being done. There are tourist subs that take people down, but they only go to a hundred metres. But in Japan they've had underwater entertainment villages with people free-diving down to get married in an air-bubble.'

Oliver laughed, and remarked, 'You know a lot about it.'

'The sea is my job,' she said simply.

She was watching the instrument panel, saw that they were near the bottom, and directed the lights downward. They came to a stop, she engaged the thrusters and glided towards the wreck. Oliver could see easily out of his porthole but had to look over her shoulder to get a forward view. The green light carved out an arc that illuminated the stricken ship. Oliver gasped at the sight of it.

'Seeing it on the video is fantastic,' he exclaimed. 'But it's nothing like this.'

More fish swam by: pink and orange sea-urchins, a barracuda, big and beautiful. Within a few inches of them shrimp and crabs scurried over rocks and buried themselves in the sand. But it was the wreck that held their eyes. With the sling round it the hull looked rather like a wounded person wrapped in bandages.

'How did you manage to do it?' Oliver asked.

For answer Dyan's right hand went to a keyboard of toggle switches which she pressed to make the manipulator arms extend and work, picking up pieces of rock and dropping them into the metal basket on the front of the sub.

'Incredible,' he murmured. 'You've all done wonderfully well.'

'Seen enough?'

'Yes.' He paused, then said, 'Thanks for bringing me down.'

Dyan spoke into the headset. 'Hal?'

'Here, boss. Ready to come up?'

'No, not yet. I'm shutting off the radio for a while. Call you later.'

'But, boss——'

Hal's voice was abruptly cut off as Dyan clicked off the switches. She took off the headset, then released the catch on her seat so that she could swivel round and face Oliver.

He was watching her, his face hard, wary. 'So this was the idea.'

'That's right.'

'Trying to scare the hell out of me, is that it?'

'No.' She shook her head. 'I wanted to talk to you. Some place where we wouldn't be disturbed.'

'Isn't this rather drastic?' he asked sarcastically.

'Possibly.'

'All right. So talk.'

'It's quite simple. I want to know just why you turned against me.'

His eyes narrowed. 'And if I don't choose to tell you?'

She shrugged. 'I can wait.'

The passenger cabin of the sub was about two metres square. A carbon dioxide scrubber droned steadily above their heads, giving them breathable air. But the water outside was very cold, making the inside of the two-inch thick titanium hull sweat cold droplets. It was dank and damp. Not a good place to be for any length of time.

After a moment Oliver said, 'All right. As you've gone to these—depths to find out, I'll tell you.' His eyes grew very cold. With certainty in his voice, he said, 'You know a man called Crispin Forster.'

Dyan's heart seemed to stop. Whatever she'd expected, it hadn't been this. Slowly she said, 'No.'

Oliver's hand shot out and gripped her wrist. 'Don't lie to me. You know him. Know him extremely well,' he added with a sneer.

'I don't know him now—I *knew* him once.'

His eyes narrowed, but Oliver sat back and let go her wrist. 'A quibble. He was your lover.'

'Yes,' she agreed, making his eyebrows rise in surprise. 'So?'

'So he just happens to be my brother-in-law!'

'Your brother-in-law?' she exclaimed in consternation. 'But—you said you weren't married.'

'I'm not. But I have a sister.'

An appalled look came into Dyan's eyes. 'And she's married to Crispin.'

'Not is—was.'

A great fear began to fill her heart. 'Is that why you came on this trip? Did you come out here looking for me? For revenge on your sister's behalf? Did you set out to make me fall in love with you, then—then use me and...?' She couldn't go on.

Oliver gave a short harsh laugh. 'No, I didn't. It was a complete coincidence. Or maybe malevolent fate,' he said bitterly. 'I was working abroad when my sister got her divorce. She couldn't bear to talk about it, so I never knew the details. Not until the day I phoned my mother on her birthday.'

Dyan's head came up. 'The day after we—we spent the night together?'

The bleak look came back into his eyes, and Oliver's mouth closed tightly for a moment, before he said, 'Yes, that morning.' He looked at her, pain in his eyes. 'Can you imagine it?' he said curtly. 'I woke up on what I thought was the happiest morning of my life. What I hoped would be the start of a whole future of happiness. I called my mother and couldn't wait to tell her that I'd found the one girl I wanted to share my life with, at long last. That I was in love and it was for keeps. And she was so happy for me——' he broke off, biting his lip '—until I told her your name.'

There was a silence as he gathered himself to go on, and Dyan was able to realise for the first time that she wasn't the only one who'd been hurt in this. He *had* been in love with her. It hadn't all been a pretence. A great weight seemed to lift from her heart and it took a moment before she could concentrate as Oliver began to speak again.

He spoke slowly, and with obvious pain, his hands balled into white-knuckled fists. 'She said that you had been responsible for the break-up of my sister's marriage. That you'd had an affair with Crispin. At first I couldn't—wouldn't—believe her. I said it had to be a mistake, that it couldn't possibly be you. But she knew what you looked like because when Jane, my sister, became suspicious of Oliver, she got my mother to hire a detective agency to follow him. The reports, the photographs, were sent to my mother and she still had them. She sent a couple of them by fax to the hotel, there and then, while I waited.' His face grew grim. 'Can you imagine what it was like, waiting, wondering?' He gave a short laugh. 'No, of course you can't.'

He paused, his jaw tight, then went on, 'When I received the copies of the photographs I knew there could be no doubt. You were the woman who had broken up my sister's marriage, ruined her life. And you were the woman I'd been fool enough to fall in love with.' His eyes had been gazing into the past, but now they came back to her, as cutting as a flick-knife. 'I knew that everything you'd done with me, you'd already done with him.'

For a moment Dyan couldn't speak, too overcome by the unfairness of life, but then she said, 'You must have known that you weren't the first man in my life.'

'Yes, I knew that,' he agreed, his voice harsh again. 'But you neglected to tell me that you'd been to bed with my brother-in-law, with a married man!'

'I didn't know,' Dyan protested.

'No, how could you know?' he agreed, to her surprise. 'But didn't it occur to you to find out before you started your sordid romance?'

She frowned, wondering how on earth she was supposed to know that she would one day meet and fall in love with Crispin's brother-in-law. 'But how could I poss——?'

But Oliver swept on, 'But why should it? What did you care if the man was married or not?' Realising they had their lines crossed, she went to interrupt, but he went on, saying with bitter contempt, 'What did you care if his wife was pregnant and expecting their first child?'

'Oh, no!'

'*Oh, yes.*' Unable to restrain himself any longer, Oliver grabbed her wrists and shook her as hard as he was able in that confined space. 'My sister,' he said fiercely, 'was head over heels in love with Crispin. She never looked at anyone else. She's gentle and loving. And she longed to have children. She'd already had a couple of miscarriages and began to be afraid that she'd never be able to carry a child. But it seemed that at last she was going to be lucky. Then she began to suspect about his affair with you. When she found out the truth she had a nervous collapse and lost that child, too.'

'Then your mother should have had more sense than to tell her,' Dyan retorted.

Oliver thrust her away from him in disgust. 'I might have guessed that would be your only reaction.'

It wasn't her only one, she had been appalled by what he'd told her, and full of pity for his sister, but Dyan had been through a great deal at his hands and she was darned if she was going to have something as terrible as this placed at her door.

'My mother did try to keep it from her,' Oliver admitted grudgingly, 'but Jane found out.' Then he said in a flat voice, that was somehow extra shocking in its lack of tone, 'It was when she lost the child that Jane tried to commit suicide.'

Dyan stared at him speechlessly for a moment, then said, hardly daring to hope, 'You said "tried"?'

'Yes. She was found in time. Unluckily for her.'

'How could it be unlucky?' Dyan asked in bewilderment.

'Because, although she was found in time to save her life, her mental breakdown was so complete that she's been in a hospital ever since,' he said heavily.

'I—I see.'

'No.' Oliver gave a bitter laugh. 'You don't see. You have no idea of the misery you've caused.'

'Well, you've certainly done your best to punish me for it. But what about Crispin? Just how did you punish him? If you could be this cruel to me, what did you do to him? Kill him?'

His face becoming a mask, Oliver said, 'He was completely devastated by what happened to Jane. He blamed himself entirely for what happened. Even though you had seduced him into the affair, he——'

'*What*?' Dyan gave an incredulous laugh. 'What the hell are you talking about?'

'You know full well,' Oliver shot back. His teeth gritting, he said, 'Crispin told my mother exactly what happened. He said he met you in America. That he'd been mugged on the street late one night, after a business dinner, and that you'd befriended him. All his money and credit-cards had been stolen so you let him stay at your apartment, gave him some drugs to kill the pain where he'd been hit. He fell asleep in your bed and when he woke in the morning you were beside him, making love to him.' He paused, seeing the disbelieving scorn in her eyes, but went on, 'After that you had a hold over him. You threatened to tell Jane if he didn't keep on with the affair. He said that you had lots of men, that you were—insatiable.'

Dyan looked at him for a long moment as he waited for her to speak, but then she began to laugh, a note of hysteria in the tone. Suddenly she stopped. 'And you really believed all that rubbish,' she said jeeringly.

'My mother believed it, yes.'

'The only part of it that's true is that I met him in America, in New York. I was in between voyages and he was there on business. But we met at a party given by a mutual acquaintance.'

'And you went to bed with him that night,' Oliver put in, his lip curling in the familiar disdain.

Looking at him, seeing the disbelief in his eyes, Dyan knew that she was never going to make him believe her side of the story. What was the point in telling him that Crispin had asked her to marry him before she went to bed with him? Oliver would never believe her for the simple reason that he didn't want to. His mother had passed on Crispin's lies and he had taken them as gospel. His love for her had turned to hate and nothing could change that now, so what was the point in defending herself? She sure as hell wasn't going to beg him to believe her.

'Believe what you like,' she said shortly. 'But your ex-brother-in-law is a liar and a cheat. I found that out for myself.' He didn't speak, just looked at her grimly, so Dyan laughed and said, 'You haven't answered the question; what did you do to him, to punish *him*?'

Oliver shook his head. 'I haven't seen him since it happened.'

Dyan's eyes widened incredulously. 'You mean to tell me that you've just accepted all that he said, taken his word for it? That you haven't even checked to see if it's true?'

A wry look came into his eyes. 'I never had the opportunity. I was away when all this happened. All I was told was that Jane and Crispin had got a divorce and that subsequently Jane had had a breakdown and gone away to recuperate. And that Crispin had taken a job abroad. I didn't know the details until I spoke to my mother on the phone that day.'

'What a warm, close family you must be,' Dyan said cuttingly.

His jaw thrusting forward, Oliver said tightly, 'It was Jane who insisted that I wasn't told. I was working on a high-level project and she didn't want me to be worried by it. And, yes, she was afraid, too, that I might show Crispin what I thought of him. Because she was still in love with him, then.'

'But they're divorced now?'

'Yes. My mother persuaded her to be rid of him.'

'And I bet he couldn't wait to go! He was the kind of man who should never have married.'

'Now that I know the full story, when I do come across him he'll wish like hell that he'd never married *my* sister,' Oliver said forcefully.

'Oh, wow! Real caveman stuff,' Dyan said mockingly. 'Be careful; he might be more difficult to hurt than a defenceless girl.'

Oliver's hand bunched into fists. 'Oh, I don't know. But then, you did know him very well.'

'Yes, I did. Much better than I knew you,' she said tauntingly.

His knuckles whitened. 'And liked him a lot better, I suppose?'

'Well, you were certainly a lot easier to like before I got to know you.'

His eyes bleak and his voice bitter, Oliver said, 'I was in love with you. I'd found the woman I'd been waiting for all my life. But then I found out what you were, had to listen to it all, had to imagine you with him—with countless other men...' His eyes filled with mingled self-disgust and pain. 'I even wanted to marry you!'

Dyan looked at him for a moment, her heart too shocked and frozen by it all to weep for the might-have-been. Then she gave a harsh laugh, 'Marry you! I'd rather die an old maid!'

Swinging her seat around, she flicked on the radio switches. 'Hal? Bring us up.'

CHAPTER EIGHT

THE submersible broke the surface and was hauled aboard the mother ship. Dyan got out first and walked across to talk to Hal. 'We'll start the lift first thing in the morning, so long as the weather is right.'

'OK, boss.' Hal looked across at Oliver as he hoisted himself out of the sub. 'Did you get what you wanted?'

Dyan didn't follow his glance. 'Yes, I suppose I did.' Turning away, she went down to her cabin, thinking that she had achieved her objective; she had at last found out why Oliver had turned against her. And just to know that there actually *was* a reason, was a great comfort. And to know that Oliver had really been in love with her, not just using her, that was a great boost to her morale, too. But, although those things gave comfort to her bruised spirit, no way did they make for happiness, or even relieve her sadness very much.

Oliver had had no hesitation in believing Crispin's lies, passed on through his mother. He preferred to believe a rejected man's malice rather than the love he felt for her. But then, Crispin was a very plausible and, she now realised, accomplished liar. Why, she herself had believed his lies for months, would have sworn that he was in love with her and that there was no other woman in his life. It was only when she had started making wedding plans, and wanted to put the announcement in the papers, that he had finally confessed the truth. At about the same time, she guessed, that his wife must have found out. Dyan gave a twisted smile; how devastating for Crispin, to have both his women turn on him at once. Unless he had another woman, tucked away somewhere, that he was cheating on, too.

But thinking about Crispin and his lies didn't help. But then, neither did thinking about Oliver. He'd said he'd been in love with her, but it hadn't been strong enough to withstand this, so what hope was there for them? None, as far as Dyan could see. Tomorrow, with any luck, the lift would take place successfully. They would sail to the nearest port and Oliver would leave, his task completed, her life wrecked. And, yes, perhaps his wrecked, too, for a while. But he would have the satisfaction of knowing that he'd punished her for what he thought she'd done; that should comfort his lonely nights. Till he met someone else. With a sigh, Dyan went up to the ops room to write up her daily report and get the latest weather forecasts.

Afterwards, Dyan took the forecasts up to Russ on the bridge. He glanced at them, then said, 'I hear you took Balfour down in the sub. Did it do any good?'

'I learnt what I wanted to know, yes.'

Russ leaned on the rail, checked that there was no one within earshot. 'Want to tell me?'

Dyan sighed. 'He's Crispin Forster's brother-in-law. Crispin was married to his sister, and the whole thing's a terrible mess.' She went on to tell him about Oliver's birthday phone call to his mother and the appalling consequences of it.

Russ listened till she'd finished, then frowned. 'Didn't you tell him Forster was lying through his teeth?'

'Yes, but he didn't believe me.'

'Not even when you told him you didn't know the guy was married? That you ditched him the minute you found out?'

She shook her head and said bitterly, 'I didn't even bother to tell him that. What would have been the point? Oliver still wouldn't have believed me. And anyway, what does it matter now? It's over—what there was of it.'

He gave her a keen look under his shaggy eyebrows. 'But you're still in love with the guy.'

'No,' Dyan answered, much too quickly. 'I couldn't care less about him.' She glanced at her watch. 'I'd better finish my work before dinner. The sooner we get the *Xanadu* and that safe on board and put ashore, the happier I'll be.' She gave a small, defeated laugh. 'In more ways than one.'

Russ watched her go, and swore under his breath, an angry frown gathering between his brows.

That evening, Dyan would have preferred to go straight to her cabin after dinner, but Russ was in a jovial mood and organised an arm-wrestling competition, insisting that Dyan hold all the betting stakes. Oliver was there, apparently content to watch, but Russ challenged him to take part. A flicker of first surprise, then wariness ran through Oliver's eyes, but he accepted the challenge without hesitation.

'Who's my opponent?' he asked lightly as he took his place at the table.

'I am.' There was a cheer from the crew as Russ took his place and Dyan was kept very busy for several minutes taking bets, most of which, she noticed, were on Russ to win. Which was hardly surprising; Russ was so strong and powerful that he always won, and had such a reputation that nowadays no one would take him on. Usually the skipper didn't issue any challenges, content in the glow of past successes, but it seemed that tonight was an exception. To teach Oliver a lesson, Dyan supposed with mixed feelings.

The two men rolled up their shirt sleeves; Russ's arm hairy, Oliver's smooth, but both muscular. Dyan found that she didn't want to watch Oliver being made to look a fool, but somehow couldn't help herself. They put their right elbows on the table, took a grip of each other's hand.

'Best of three. Give the word, Logan,' Russ growled out.

'Are you both ready?' she said in a strained voice.

'Ready.' They spoke together.

'Go!'

Their muscles tightened and knuckles showed white as both men exerted their strength. The crew were expecting a quick result, and were surprised when Russ didn't immediately force Oliver's arm down. They began to shout words of encouragement and let out a cheer as Russ slowly, very slowly bent Oliver's arm towards the table and finally held it there.

Both men took a drink and rested a moment before they gripped hands for the second time. Again Dyan gave them the start, and the men shouted for Russ, confident of another easy victory. But Oliver's face hardened with effort, his lips drawn back as he put all his strength into it. Slowly he began to dominate. The men renewed their shouts, but this time it was Russ's arm that was forced down to the table's surface. Dyan wondered fleetingly if Russ had allowed him to win, for some reason, but there was sweat on the older man's face, his skin red with effort.

Giving Oliver a look of surprised respect, Russ said, 'So it looks as if I'm defending my title.'

'Your title?'

'He's the arm-wrestling champion of Starr Marine,' someone told him excitedly.

Oliver looked amused. 'Is he, now? Thanks for getting round to telling me.'

Again the two squared up to each other, and this time the match was really close. All the men were shouting and cheering for Russ, but Dyan just sat and held her breath, her eyes riveted on them as they put every last ounce of strength into the contest. That it was taking all their strength was very obvious; their breath was harsh and panting, the veins in their arms standing out with effort, their whole beings concentrated entirely on beating the other. Russ's arm, fraction by fraction of an inch, began to move towards the table. At first the men went on shouting encouragement, but then they fell silent as it came home to them that their champion was about to be defeated, and by an outsider, a man they already had cause to dislike. Russ's arm, no matter how much he fought against it, came within a couple of inches of the table. But suddenly, to everyone's amazement, Oliver's strength seemed to give out and it was his arm that was swung over and hit the table instead!

The room erupted into great cheers as men who had seen their bets lost, their champion disgraced, suddenly had everything come right again. The two contestants, though, sat in silence. They were still eye-to-eye, a tight-lipped look on Russ's face, a small smile on that of Oliver. 'Congratulations,' the latter said, and put a hand on Russ's shoulder as he got to his feet, then went out of the cabin.

A hubbub of excited talk broke out, Russ was thumped on the back.

'You broke him nicely, Skipper.'

'Bet he thought he was going to win, but you showed him, Skipper.'

But Russ shook off the congratulations and went to the bar to get himself a drink while the men crowded round Dyan to collect their winnings.

The crowd of people, the men's excitement, had made the cabin unbearably hot. When she'd given out the last winnings, Dyan went up on deck to cool off. Automatically she glanced up at the sky, saw it clear and dark, pricked with stars, the moon dazzlingly bright; the sort of night Oliver said he would like to have given her on that night they'd made love. But then it had rained and thundered. It should have been an omen, that storm, Dyan thought wryly. She walked along the deck away from the companion-way and the bridge, wondering where Oliver was, whether he was still smarting from his defeat. He had left the galley soon enough, rather than face the men; but then, she already knew he was a poor loser.

She passed into the shadow of the lifeboat and there was a soft footfall. Dyan turned but was unable to see who it was before a man caught hold of her and pulled her roughly into his arms. She thought it was Oliver, trying to punish her by seducing her again, and gave an angry cry. But almost immediately she knew it wasn't him; this man wasn't so tall and smelt of tobacco. One of the crew, then. And it didn't take much guessing to know which one.

As he tried to kiss her, she managed to push him away a little and say, 'Dave! Let go. I mean it. I——'

But he bent her back and forced his mouth on hers, his breath disgusting from whisky and cigarettes. Furiously angry, most of all because it meant that he had no respect for her as his boss, Dyan got her hands on his chest and forced him away again.

'You louse! Get off me.'

But he put a hand in her hair and said thickly, 'You know you want it. You gave it to Balfour, why not to me?'

Again he tried to kiss her and Dyan realised she would have to make him let her go. But before she could do so Dave seemed to be suddenly plucked away from her. There was the sound of a fist meeting skin. Dave went sprawling and then Oliver said viciously, 'Touch her again, creep, and I'll kick you over the side.'

Dave picked himself up, was about to say something, but saw the look in Oliver's eyes and thought better of it. Cursing, he took himself off.

'Are you all right?' Oliver asked.

'No, I am not all right,' Dyan said furiously. 'How *dare* you interfere? I was quite capable of getting rid of him.'

'So why didn't you?'

'I was just about to when you came along.'

'Really?' he said sceptically. 'How?'

'I've taken lessons in self-defence; I could have handled him easily, especially as he was half drunk. Although if it hadn't been for you he wouldn't have tried at all!'

'Now wait a minute; you can't blame that on me.'

'Oh, can't I? If he hadn't seen you treating me like dirt, he wouldn't have thought that he could, too. Now he has no respect for me, but I could have got it back by getting the better of him if you hadn't decided to do your macho act again. Now he'll think that I have to have a man to protect me,' she finished in disgust.

'I beg your pardon,' Oliver said stiffly, adding sarcastically, 'Next time I'll just walk by.'

'Yes, you do that,' she agreed furiously. She began to walk away, then suddenly swung round on him. 'I thought I still had the respect of the men, that I had that left at least. But now you've taken even that away from me. You should be very satisfied, very happy. You've got it all! I've nothing left now.' Turning, she ran down the deck, away from him, left him staring after her.

Preparations for the lift began at first light the next morning. Hal went down with one of the other divers, but Dave kept well out of the way. When someone asked him at breakfast how he got his swollen jaw, he muttered something about tripping over. As everyone knew he'd had a lot to drink, his explanation was accepted, and Dyan just hoped he had enough sense to keep his mouth shut.

It took nearly the whole day to raise the wreck. It was brought slowly to the surface, the submersible reporting progress from below until it was near enough for the divers to go down in frogmen's suits to oversee the final hoist aboard the *Guiding Starr*. Dyan watched the video screens anxiously, continuously afraid that the weight of the safe would spoil all their efforts. But the men had done a good job; the airbags gave it sufficient buoyancy and the slings held. When the superstructure finally broke the surface a great cheer went up from all the men and Dyan came racing on deck to see.

It took another couple of hours then to hoist it aboard the mother ship, and only then did she relax in relief. The job was done. Oliver's firm would retrieve their insurance money on the boat, the pop star would get his *objets d'art* back and Barney would get paid for the job. Everyone would be happy—with the exception of herself, Dyan thought in sudden weariness at the relaxation of tension.

When the *Xanadu* was safely lashed to the deck Russ came down to have a look. 'Where's this safe I've heard so much about?'

'I'll show you.' Dyan took him aboard the boat, but raised her eyebrows in surprise when Russ invited Oliver to come along.

If felt eerie walking across a deck slippery with seaweed, going into cabins that had such a short time ago been under water. They had taken the airbags out and the boat was propped up so that it was on an even keel.

'It's in here.' She led them through the main cabin and into the heart of the boat. The safe, almost as big as a room, took up most of the space. 'It's waterproof, so the things inside should be OK. Unless any of them have fallen and broken, of course. But we won't be able to find that out until whoever has the key opens it.'

'It doesn't need a key,' Oliver remarked. 'It has a time-lock.'

'You mean the door has been opening while it's been under the sea?' Dyan asked in amazement.

'No. You see this sort of flap in the door here,' Oliver said, pointing. 'At certain times of the day that unlocks itself, and if someone wants to use the safe the flap can be pushed aside. Inside there's a digital display. If the right combination of numbers is fed into it the actual door of the safe will open.'

'But will it still work after it's been underwater for so long?' Russ asked.

'Oh, yes. It has energy cells inside that would make it go on working indefinitely.'

'Won't the sea have got under the flap?'

'No, that has a waterproof seal. We insisted on that before we would insure it.'

'Ingenious,' Dyan remarked. 'So the safe can only be opened by someone who knows the combination. Who's that—the pop star?'

'Yes, but I know it as well. And——' he looked at his watch '—allowing for the time difference, I think we'll be able to open the safe and make sure the contents are OK at about dawn tomorrow.'

'You're going to open it?' Russ asked.

Oliver nodded. 'I have a list of what's supposed to be in it and I want to check that it's correct.' He smiled. 'Coming along to have a look, Skipper?'

'I wouldn't miss it,' Russ declared.

'Dyan, I need to go through the inventory; will you act as a witness, please?'

'Oh, sure.' She gave a bitter little smile. 'I might as well see what I've gone through all this to find.' She shivered and turned away. 'I want to get out into the sun again; this boat gives me the creeps.'

Russ led the way, but when they went through the main cabin, he stopped to look around. 'Hey,' he exclaimed, bending to pick up a bracelet from where it had fallen from a drawer that had flown open during the lift. 'This looks something like the bracelet Forster gave you.'

Dyan's heart froze, and she grew very still, but behind her Oliver said, 'Forster?'

'Yeah,' Russ replied. 'The guy Dyan used to be engaged to.'

His eyes narrowing, Oliver said, 'You know him?'

'Sure, we all knew him. They were going around together for months after they got engaged. We used to have bets on whether or not he would be waiting on the dock every time we put into port. He was nearly always there.'

'Has Dyan told you about my relationship to him?' Oliver demanded.

'Yeah, she has. And I think it's about time someone put the record straight,' Russ answered shortly. 'That swine never told Dyan he was married. She thought he was free. He even asked her to marry him and gave her an engagement ring, as well as a bracelet,' he said, tossing the one in his hand back on the floor. 'And the only reason he did that was to get her to go to bed with him.'

'Russ, please,' Dyan begged, her face flaming.

But the captain went on, 'It wasn't until she started making plans for the wedding that he told her the truth. She ditched him then, as soon as she found out, but he tried to keep her on a string by saying he was getting a divorce. But Dyan wouldn't have anything to do with him after that. She's no homewrecker; anyone who's got a grain of sense ought to be able to see that.'

Embarrassed beyond bearing, Dyan tried to walk past him out the door, but he put his large bulk in the opening and barred the way.

'If all this is true, why didn't she tell me so herself?' Oliver demanded.

'Because she's too darn proud, that's why,' Russ said angrily.

'Will you please stop talking about me as if I'm not here?' Dyan said furiously. 'You had no right to say anything, Russ. This is nothing to do with you. All you've done is waste your own time and embarrass me. Now get out of my way.' For a moment he didn't move, a stubborn look to his mouth, but she snapped out, 'That's an order, Captain.'

He grinned and moved aside, and she hurried on to the deck of the *Guiding Starr*. But, behind her, Oliver said, 'Dyan, could I talk to you a moment?'

'Is it about the *Xanadu* and its contents?'

He gave her a troubled look. 'No, I——'

She saw that it was personal, so quickly said, 'No. You've nothing to say that I want to hear, and I certainly have nothing to say to you.'

Again she turned and strode away, and when he called, 'Wait,' she took no notice. He followed her to the ops room but she went into the office, closed the door, and pointedly picked up the phone. Oliver stood there for a moment, then turned and walked away.

After she'd phoned Barney to tell him the good news, Dyan went up to the bridge to see Russ. Still angry, she got him alone and said, 'Why did you tell him? What I said to you was in confidence. You had no right to interfere.'

'Simmer down, Logan. Somebody had to put him straight.'

'Why? What's the point?'

'Do you want him to go on hating you? Wouldn't you rather he understood?'

'I don't care how he feels about me.'

Russ put a hand on her shoulder. 'Yes, you do.'

She shook her head. 'No. Not any more.' She raised bleak eyes to his. 'And can't you see that it isn't any use? The very fact that I've been with his brother-in-law will always make him hate me.'

'You don't know that. Give him a chance to——'

'Yes, I do know,' Dyan interrupted fiercely. 'And even if his feelings towards me did change, do you really think that I'd want him now, after what he's done to me?'

'When men are deeply in love, and something goes wrong, then they do crazy things, Logan. Things they often regret.'

'So let him regret it,' Dyan said tartly. 'I couldn't care less. And anyway, I don't see why you're sticking up for him. You hate poor losers, and after the way he just walked out of the cabin last night after you beat him at arm-wrestling, I'm surprised you——'

'I didn't beat him. He let me win,' Russ said shortly, and nodded as her eyes widened. 'That's right. He let me keep the men's respect.' He smiled slightly. 'And the men their money. And he went out straight away so that I wouldn't have the opportunity to tell them all.'

She gave a troubled frown. 'Are you sure? It looked as if you'd been playing with him.'

'Of course I'm sure. He made it look that way. I would have been beaten fair and square.'

'But why did he do it?'

'I've told you why. He, at least, has some respect for my grey hairs. And I was right about him in the first place, Logan. First impressions usually are. He's OK. Give him a chance.'

But, recognising his allusion, she said, 'I'm sorry if I pulled rank on you.' Dyan lifted a heavy hand to push her hair out of her eyes. 'I'm tired. I think I'll skip supper and have an early night.'

'Think about what I said.'

She shook her head. 'There's no point—but thanks for caring, Skipper.'

'Don't forget to be up early to see the safe opened.'

'I won't.'

Back in her cabin, Dyan rang Joe and asked him to bring her a sandwich, which she ate while she worked on her report. Some time later there was a knock on the door and Oliver said, 'Dyan, please let me come in and talk to you.' But she didn't even bother to answer. He knocked again, but then went away.

Early the next morning Dyan pulled on jeans and a thick sweater, to keep out the dank eeriness of the wrecked boat as much as the morning breeze. Oliver was already waiting for her down by the *Xanadu*, but Russ was up on the bridge, handing over to the first mate as the ship headed for home. Some of the men on watch were nearby, probably hoping to have a look inside the safe themselves, Dyan guessed, and was glad that they were there when Oliver walked towards her.

'Hello, Dyan.'

'Good morning,' she answered stiffly.

'Were you asleep last night—or just refusing to answer?'

'What do you think?'

His lips tightened, but before he could say anything, Russ came striding down the deck towards them.

Immediately, Dyan turned to greet him, then said, 'Let's get this over with.'

They climbed on to the *Xanadu* and went below. There wasn't much light but Oliver and Russ had each brought a torch.

Oliver looked at his watch. 'The time-lock should be working now.' He pressed the flap and it moved smoothly to one side, as if it had never been submerged. They saw the digital display and Oliver tapped in eight numbers from memory. For a moment Dyan thought it wasn't going to work, but there was a soft click and the door to the safe swung slowly open.

'Aladdin's cave,' Oliver said, a thrill of satisfaction and excitement in his voice.

But the inside of the safe was a great anti-climax. Dyan had somehow expected all the beautiful things to be on display, but they were, of course, all carefully packed away in boxes. 'Oh!' She gave a little sound of disappointment. Oliver glanced at her, and she said wryly, 'Life is full of disillusionment; I should have remembered that.'

'And sometimes there is beauty and treasure hidden away so that you don't recognise it for what it is.' His eyes held hers, making sure she understood his meaning, but then he said, 'Like this,' and took the lid off one of the crates to reveal the most beautiful bronze statuette of a nymph playing some pipes. It was only about two feet high, but exquisitely cast, the figure full of life and movement.

Looking at it, Dyan smiled with pleasure, then gave a small chuckle. 'Maybe I'll take up pop singing.'

Both men laughed. 'Well, I've seen all there is to see, so I'll leave you to get on with checking your list,' Russ remarked.

Dyan gave him a frowning look, and said pointedly, 'Don't you want to stay? The mate can handle the ship surely?'

'I said I'd only be away for a few minutes. Maybe I'll come back later,' was the most she could get out of him.

Keeping her voice determinedly brisk, Dyan said, 'Where's your list?'

Oliver took it from his pocket. 'We can mark off that statuette. Can you see some boxed paintings? They should be marked with their names on the outside.'

'There are some over the back.' Dyan glanced at him, expecting him to go and look, but Oliver was taking out a pen and unscrewing the top. Impatiently she climbed over a couple of smaller cases and went to see for herself. She reached them and was trying to read the labels when she heard a noise behind her—and looked round to see that Oliver was pulling the door shut!

'What are you doing?'

She sprung up to stop him but it was too late; the big door clicked shut and they were in sudden, complete darkness, as if they had suddenly gone blind.

'What have you done?' Dyan exclaimed in horror.

Oliver flicked on the torch. Quite calmly he said, 'It seems that if I want to talk to you alone then I, too, must take drastic measures.'

'Are you crazy? Do you realise that we're stuck in here? That there's no way we can get out? Even if Russ opens the flap he won't know the combination. He can't open the safe and get us out. We—we'll die in here.' There was a note of appalled horror in her voice, an edge of terror.

Oliver quickly set the torch on a packing-case and pulled her to him. 'My darling girl,' he said softly. 'Do you really think I'll let you die?'

She stared at him, saw that there was no madness in his eyes, as she'd feared. 'You—you've given Russ the combination. You arranged this between you!'

'Of course.' Oliver grinned. 'But I didn't need to give him the combination. The safe-maker envisaged such an emergency as this. I can open the safe from the inside in exactly the same way as we got in, whenever I want to.'

Dyan pushed away from him in indignant rage. 'You locked me in here on purpose, damn you!'

'It was the only way I could think of to get you alone. Dyan, I *have* to talk to you. Sort this out.' He gave a grim smile. 'And now you're definitely a captive audience.'

'Do you think I'm going to listen to you after you play a dirty trick like this on me?' Dyan banged her fist angrily against the door of the safe. 'Open this door! Let me out!'

'I'm sorry. Not until we've talked.'

He waited until Dyan saw the futility of it and turned to lean against the door, her face set in mutinous lines, her arms folded across her chest in angry defiance. 'All right, so waste my time. Talk.'

For a moment he seemed to be finding the right question, but eventually said, 'When we were down in the sub and I told you about Crispin and my sister; why didn't you tell me then that he'd tricked you, that you didn't know he was married?'

'Because it wasn't of any importance. Open the door.'

'I'm not Russ; you can't order me around. So why go to the trouble of taking me down in the sub, then?'

'You know the reason; I wanted to find out why you'd turned against me. I wanted to find out whether something had happened, or whether you were just the kind of man who enjoyed making a woman fall for him, but then turned on her,' she snapped out. 'So now you know, so open the door.'

'Shortly.' Oliver gave a rueful sigh. 'It seems I owe you a big apology.'

'Save it. I'm not interested.'

But he went on, 'You see, I was so much in love with you, completely crazy about you. And when I found out about Crispin I think I went *really* crazy for a while. I was happier than I'd ever been in my life—but suddenly everything went smashing down to the ground in ruins. I was completely devastated. God, I've never felt like that before. My love for you, all my emotions, seemed to go spinning out of control. I was so *angry*! And I took that anger out on you. I lost all sense of proportion. I wanted to hurt you because my own hurt was so bad, the pain so deep.' He bunched his hands in memory. His face was taut and a pulse beat in his temple. Slowly he lifted his eyes to look at her. 'Can you understand, Dyan? Can you imagine what it did to me?'

She stood staring at him, her arms still folded, but wrapped around herself. 'Of course I can,' she said shortly. 'How the hell do you think I've been feeling these last weeks?'

'I was wrong about you, and I'm terribly, terribly sorry. If I'd been thinking straight I would have realised that someone as wonderful as you wouldn't go with——'

'Look, just forget it. It doesn't matter any more.'

'Of course it damn well matters,' Oliver said forcefully. 'Because I'm still in love with you. Because that never really changed. No matter how angry I was, no matter what I did to you, I was always in love with you. Nothing could change that. Not now or ever.'

Dyan gazed into his eyes for a long moment, saw there that he spoke with utter sincerity. But she turned away. 'You're too late,' she said shortly. 'I couldn't care less how you feel. Now open the door.'

'I know you're angry. You have every reason to be. And I was a fool not to follow my first instincts, not to believe in you. Would it help,' he asked earnestly, 'if I spent the rest of my life making it up to you?'

She swung her head round to stare at him, and he reached out and caught her hand. Immediately she tried to take it back, but Oliver held it fast. 'Will you please let go? I've already told you I couldn't care less about you.'

'But I somehow don't believe you.'

'Well, you'd better believe it, because——' She broke off as he drew her nearer and she saw the look of determination in his eyes. 'No!'

But he pulled her into his arms and smothered her protests with his mouth, stopped the angry words with kisses, drowned all resistance with the rightness of being back in his arms again.

It was a long time before he let her go, and then he only did so because he felt the wetness of her tears on his skin.

'Dyan?' He held her away from him, anxiety in his face. 'Oh, my dear! Can you still not forgive me?'

She shook her head. 'It wouldn't work. You're sorry now, but it will always be there—between us.'

A devastated look came into Oliver's eyes. 'Have I hurt you so badly, then? Is there nothing I can say——?'

'No, not that.' She shook her head, then said painfully, 'You'll always remember that I've—that Crispin and I...'

Lifting his hands, Oliver put them on either side of her face and looked at her with utmost sincerity, willing her to believe him. 'That isn't so. I'm over that. I've realised that I'll always love you, no matter what. I'm not jealous of your past, just eager to share your future.'

'Can you really forget him?'

He gave a grim smile. 'I will be able to once I've found him and given him what he deserves for ruining my sister's life, for making you so unhappy.'

'Oh, I'm all for that. But what about your family? They won't be able to——'

'My family,' Oliver interrupted firmly, 'will soon learn to love you as much as I do, once they know the truth.' He looked at her earnestly. 'I love you so much, Dyan. Besides that nothing else matters. I know that now. Please say you'll marry me?'

She looked at him for a long moment, then drew his hands down. A look of bleak dejection came into his face, and deepened as she said, 'I shall never forgive you.' And then deliberately paused before adding, 'For proposing to me in such a terrible place.'

His eyes widened, stared in sudden, brilliant hope.

Dyan laughed and nodded, tears in her eyes again. 'Of course I'll marry you, you idiot.' And she went happily into his arms, where she belonged.

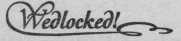

HARLEQUIN 🛡 PRESENTS®

Ever felt the excitement of forbidden fruit?
Ever been thrilled by feverish desire?

Then you'll enjoy our selection of
dangerously sensual stories.

Take a chance on

Dangerous Liaisons

Falling in love is a risky affair!

Watch for:

#1818 FLIRTING WITH DANGER
by Kate Walker

Who was the good guy, who was her secret admirer...
were they one and the same man?

Available in June wherever Harlequin books are sold.

DL-F

UNLOCK THE DOOR TO GREAT ROMANCE
AT BRIDE'S BAY RESORT

Join Harlequin's new across-the-lines series, set in an exclusive hotel on an island off the coast of South Carolina.

Seven of your favorite authors will bring you exciting stories about fascinating heroes and heroines discovering love at Bride's Bay Resort.

Look for these fabulous stories coming to a store near you beginning in January 1996.

Harlequin American Romance #613 in January
Matchmaking Baby by Cathy Gillen Thacker

Harlequin Presents #1794 in February
Indiscretions by Robyn Donald

Harlequin Intrigue #362 in March
Love and Lies by Dawn Stewardson

Harlequin Romance #3404 in April
Make Believe Engagement by Day Leclaire

Harlequin Temptation #588 in May
Stranger in the Night by Roseanne Williams

Harlequin Superromance #695 in June
Married to a Stranger by Connie Bennett

Harlequin Historicals #324 in July
Dulcie's Gift by Ruth Langan

Visit Bride's Bay Resort each month wherever Harlequin books are sold.

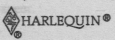